My Little Sister's a ZOMBIE!

Mike Catalano

Jason Bailey

OTHER LIVING DEAD PRESS BOOKS

MY LITTLE SISTER'S A
ZOMBIE!

WRITTEN BY
MIKE CATALANO

ILLUSTRATED BY
JASON BAILEY

DEDICATION from Jason:
For Kaitlyn Paige —
The most incredible little girl, who has brought so much love and
inspiration to my life.
For Logan — An extraordinary son and big brother, who makes me
proud every day!

DEDICATION from Mike:
For Joe and Henry — You guys always keep me smiling with such
content amazement. I'm honored to be your Daddy!

MY LITTLE SISTER'S A ZOMBIE!

For it has been deemed, one Halloween night,
A child shall be born of an unnatural sight,
And those that look on shall earn their fright,
But beware most of all... the odd appetite.

- 1 -

On most days, the town of Hallowed Hills was a lot like any other tucked-away community off the interstate.

People would say "hi" while passing on the street, homes had freshly cut lawns, and birds would tweet from atop tall trees. That was how things worked on most sunny days.

However, there were also those other, lesser frequent days. The kinds of days that set Hallowed Hills apart from any place you could possibly imagine. See, once in a while, a dark cloud would settle over the town and cast a spell of strangeness that just could not be explained.

People would still go about their daily business, and never thought twice about looking over their shoulders. Because whenever a dark cloud set up shop in the sky, you never knew what eerie oddity would sprout up on the hills.

Dressed in a cowboy Halloween costume and holding a shiny toy pistol in both hands, Logan squirmed in his seat in the waiting room of Hallowed Hills General Hospital.

He tapped the barrels of the six-shooters against his seat.

"What's the matter, Logan?" his grandma asked.

"When will the baby get here?" Logan asked. "I want my baby brother!"

"Hopefully soon... and how do you know the baby will be a boy?"

"Because I want one!"

Logan held up his pistols.

"See," he began, "I even brought him a gun so we could play 'shoot the bad guy' when he gets here! We're going to play lots of games together!"

Logan aimed his pistols at a pumpkin-headed scarecrow decoration and fired off a couple of fake rounds.

"Well, your brother will be here soon," his grandma smiled and kissed him on the forehead.

Logan playfully wiped off the kiss and brought the pistols back to his seat.

He resumed the impatient tapping. Outside the waiting room's windows, he could see numerous costumed children scampering along the sidewalk, joyfully swinging their bags of trick-or-treat prizes.

Missing out on the door-to-door action didn't bother him much.

He was more excited for the big prize that was about to come out from his mom's large, round tummy.

Suddenly, Logan's dad rushed into the waiting room. Grandma and Logan jumped off their seats in anticipation.

"Great news!" Dad exclaimed. "She's here!"

Grandma let out a cheer and gave Dad a hug. Logan remained standing with a confused expression. Dad walked up to him.

"What's up, buddy?" he asked kneeling down.

"Who's she?" Logan asked.

"She's your newborn baby sister."

Logan's eyes bulged wide.

He dropped his pistols to the floor and his mouth hung open for a second before uttering, "My sister?"

- 3 -

Holding onto a pink balloon that read, **It's a Girl**, Logan followed his dad into room number 303 in the maternity ward of the hospital. His mom was sitting up on a bed, holding a tiny baby wrapped up in a white blanket. She was sweaty and looked very tired, but happy. Her smile had a slightly calming effect on Logan.

"Come here, Logan," Mom said. "Meet your baby sister."

"I don't need to, Mommy," Logan replied.

"Don't be silly, buddy," Dad said and picked Logan up. "Let's go say hi."

Logan fidgeted a bit anxiously as his dad held him up above his mom and the baby. The blanket covered most of his newborn sister's face.

"Okay, Logan," Mom said. "Here's your sister, Kaitlyn."

Mom unwrapped the blanket, revealing a small pinkish face. The baby was sleeping.

"Go ahead, Logan," Dad said, leaning him closer. "Say hello."

Logan slowly reached out his hand and touched Kaitlyn's dark hair. Her eyes at once popped open. Startled, Logan pulled back toward his father.

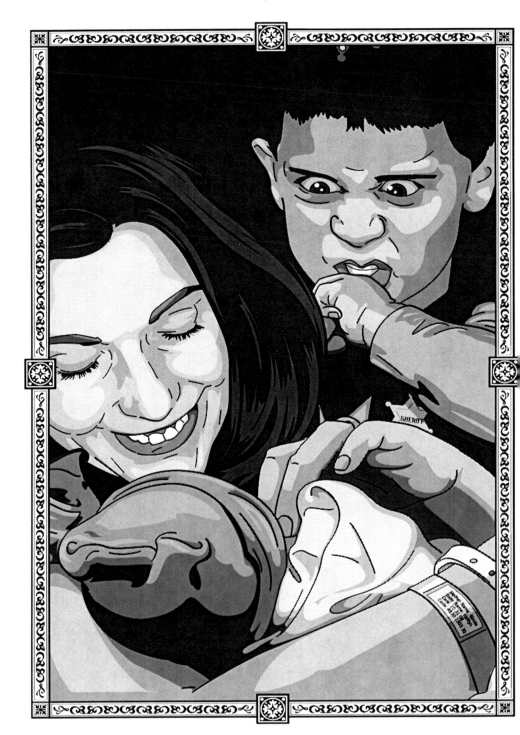

"Look, she's awake!" Mom smiled. "I told you she wanted to meet you."

Logan stared at Kaitlyn. She had the shiniest eyes he had ever seen.

"Her eyes are glowing," he said.

"Aw, how cute," Mom said.

Kaitlyn lifted up her teeny hand from the blanket toward Logan.

"She knows you're her big brother," Dad said.

Logan laughed and stretched his hand out to Kaitlyn's. The baby wrapped her pudgy fingers around his index finger and slowly pulled him closer. Her skin turned a darker shade of pink as she opened her mouth. She had a very strong grip.

"Is she yawning?" Logan asked.

Kaitlyn opened her mouth wider and quickly shoved Logan's finger in past her toothless gums.

"Ah!" Logan screamed and yanked his hand out of her grasp. "She tried to bite me!"

-4-

From that Halloween on, Logan was saddled with a sister. With his dreams of a baby brother now dashed, he quietly returned to his fairly-normal life as a kid, leaving all Kaitlyn-related tasks to his mom and dad. After all, it wasn't as if a boy as young as he was could be expected to change diapers or feed bottles in the middle of the night.

Still, even simple things, like posing for a picture with Kaitlyn or getting her a rattle, were never very high on Logan's *fun things to do* list.

He also never fully got past their initial introduction when Kaitlyn mistook his finger for a chicken nugget. Even though that little baby had yet to grow teeth, her jaw sure seemed to be packing some big-time crushing power. And he didn't feel like getting too close once Kaitlyn began developing actual chompers.

He really worked at keeping his distance from Kaitlyn after she began displaying some strange behavior at her one year old birthday party.

After everyone sang "Happy Birthday," she just gazed quietly at the cake with a little #1 candle on top of it, her skin becoming a darker shade of pink. She then pro-ceeded to smash her entire face into the cake and take a huge bite, candle and all.

Everyone at the party thought her action was very cute and funny, but not Logan. He knew that the glow in her eyes was not simply the reflection from the candle.

The only problem was that he seemed to be the only one to know this. So that night, he snuck into her bedroom, hoping to find some evidence in his favor.

Kaitlyn was asleep in her crib with a pink blanket covering much of her face. Logan peered down at her, wondering what color her skin was.

He reached out toward the blanket. All of a sudden, the pink cover popped up in the crib like a ghost. Surprised, he fell backwards onto the floor.

The blanket fell to the base of the crib, revealing Kaitlyn and her glowing eyes.

Logan jumped to his feet and ran out of the bedroom, slamming the door closed behind him.

- 5 -

Seated on the floor before a couch in the living room, Logan and his best friend, Joe, were in the middle of an intense racecar video game. Their thumbs moved frantically over the wireless controllers in their hands.

"Watch out for the oil on the track!" Logan shouted.

"I got it, I got it," Joe answered.

Mom poked her head inside the living room. She held a sleeping Kaitlyn in her arms. Although Kaitlyn was now three years old, she still clung to her mother like she was still a newborn.

"You two having fun?" Mom asked, walking over to a cushioned playpen.

"Yeah, Mom," Logan said, keeping his eyes on the television.

"Good. I'm going to go check on Dad in the backyard. Kaitlyn just fell asleep. Will you just keep an eye on her for me?"

"Aw, Mom, she's three years old now. Can't she take care of herself?" Logan whined.

"No, I'd like you to do it because you're a very responsible seven year old. Right, Logan? A very responsible seven year old who gets to play fun video games?"

Logan rolled his eyes and answered, "Okay, Mom. I'll watch her."

"Very good. I knew I could count on you to make the right decision."

Mom placed Kaitlyn down inside the playpen.

"I'll be right outside if you need anything," she said and ducked out of the living room.

With his eyes still glued to the television, Logan said, "Kaitlyn, stay asleep and don't do anything while we're playing right now. This is a very important race."

As the two boys continued their electronic racing, Kaitlyn perked up her head and glanced out of the playpen at them. She slowly placed her hand at the top edge and climbed out onto the arm of the couch. Logan and Joe didn't notice her.

Kaitlyn's skin turned a very dark shade of pink. She hopped onto the seat cushion directly behind Joe and opened her mouth to reveal an upper and lower row of shiny, sharp teeth.

"I see the finish line!" Logan cried out.

"Hit the gas!" Joe exclaimed.

"I'm going as fast as I can!"

Suddenly, Kaitlyn leapt off the couch and landed on top of Joe's back. Joe dropped his controller and screamed. Logan looked at his friend in dismay.

"Get her off me!" Joe screamed.

Kaitlyn held onto Joe's shoulders, her skin now nearly purple, her toothy mouth wide open.

"Kaitlyn!" Logan yelled. "No!"

Kaitlyn looked up at her brother.

"Hun-gy," she said in her baby-ish voice and went to bite Joe.

"Stop!" Logan said and threw his controller at her.

The controller hit Kaitlyn in the side of the head and knocked her off Joe. Logan jumped to his feet and yanked his friend out of her reach.

"I'm going home!" Joe shouted and ran out of the living room.

"Joe, wait!" Logan called.

His friend did not answer him. Logan was all alone in the living room... with Kaitlyn. He shot a glance to the base of the couch. She wasn't there. His ears detected a low growling noise. He spun around to see his baby sister crouching atop the television, her eyes glowing green.

"Kaitlyn!" Logan shouted. "Get down!"

Kaitlyn grinned and jumped off the television. She landed with a thud and immediately darted at Logan.

"Whoa!" Logan yelled and ran out of the living room and into the kitchen.

Kaitlyn charged after him, like a rabid puppy dog, on all fours. She was very fast and slid into the refrigerator, causing it to open. Logan tried running for the back door that led to the backyard, but Kaitlyn cut him off. He abruptly turned around and ended up slipping on the tiled floor. He landed on his butt and began backing away from his baby sister.

"Hun-gy," Kaitlyn smiled and sprinted forward.

Logan moved backwards as fast as possible until he hit the opened refrigerator. A package of hot dogs fell out and hit him on the head.

Kaitlyn was getting closer and closer. Unsure of what else to do, Logan reached into the package and began hurling hot dogs at her. The flying wieners bopped Kaitlyn in the chest.

"Oh, no," Logan said upon realizing he was down to his last hot dog.

Aiming for Kaitlyn's face, he threw the hot dog as hard as he could. It went spinning through the air and connected with her jaw.

Kaitlyn actually caught it in her mouth and stopped in her tracks.

She started chewing and soon the hot dog was gone. Pleased, she bent down and picked up another and gobbled it up.

Her purple skin began returning to its pink-ish color as she continued eating up all the hot dogs on the floor.

Logan was too nervous to interrupt her. He merely stayed seated against the opened refrigerator until she was finished.

"Kaitlyn, you're not supposed to eat those," Logan said cautiously.

Kaitlyn just stared at him and smiled. Her eyes no longer glowed green.

"Tank-you," she said and walked out of the kitchen.

That night, Logan had trouble going to sleep. The odd *'Kaitlyn attack'* weighed heavily on his mind as he wrestled beneath his bedcovers. To make matters worse, he'd lost his videogame privileges as punishment for accidentally giving Kaitlyn a small bruise on the side of her head.

He wanted to tell his parents exactly how she had gotten the bruise, but was afraid they wouldn't believe him, which would lead to further punishment for lying. He also did not want to get reprimanded for feeding his baby sister hot dogs.

After exhausting all possible scenarios of the past day, Logan's mind finally stopped thinking and allowed him to go to sleep. His body was finally at rest when something pushed down on his stomach.

The pressure stirred him out of his slumber. He opened his eyes to find a small figure standing on top of him. The glowing eyes in the pitch-black room were a dead giveaway as to who it was.

"Kaitlyn!" he softly shouted in shock.

"Hun-gy!" his sister said.

"Don't eat *me!*"

Logan slid out of the covers and scuttled back to the bed's headboard. He grabbed his pillow and held it in

front of him like a shield. Kaitlyn turned her head to the side, confused.

"Hun-gy!" she repeated.

"Go back to your room," Logan nervously ordered, looking for something else to defend himself with.

"No room. Hun-gy!"

Kaitlyn's tummy let out a loud growl and Logan's fear slightly lessened.

"You want to eat *something*?" he asked.

Kaitlyn nodded. Logan slowly lowered his pillow.

"Okay, then I'll try to get you something to eat," he said. "Other than me, that is. Come on, let's go downstairs."

Logan jumped off his bed and grabbed his pee-wee football helmet and shoulder pads. While walking toward the door, he threw on the gear and looked back at his sister, who was still sitting on the bed.

"Come on, Kaitlyn," he said, waving his hand over. "Let's get you a snack before Mom and Dad wake up."

At once, Kaitlyn hopped off the bed and dashed toward him. They entered the dark upstairs hallway together.

"You're like a puppy," Logan laughed.

Kaitlyn leapt up and switched on the hall light.

"No!" Logan whispered harshly.

He dove forward and turned the switch off.

"If you turn on the light, Kaitlyn, everyone will know where we are. Remember that."

"So-wee, *Wo-gan*."

Downstairs, Logan and Kaitlyn snuck into the dark kitchen. He opened the refrigerator door. The light from inside illuminated the tiled floor. Logan could see that Kaitlyn was beginning to turn purple again.

"Oh no!" he exclaimed. "We better hurry!"

He glanced inside the fridge. He shoved a couple of items out of the way and found a container of leftover meatballs. He opened the lid so fast, that a couple of meatballs popped out onto the floor. Kaitlyn quickly scooped them up in her mouth and nearly swallowed them whole.

"Whoa, be careful," Logan said. "Do you want any more?"

Kaitlyn nodded. Logan took out another meatball and held it out. His baby sister opened her mouth and stepped forward. Remembering what happened the last time his hand got close to her mouth, he yanked back the meatball and instead tossed it up in the air.

Kaitlyn stood right under the falling meaty meteor and caught it in between her sharp teeth. She ground it up with glee as her skin tone switched back to pink.

"Are you full now?" Logan asked, dangling a piece of steak over her.

Kaitlyn walked up to her big brother and gave him a small hug.

"Tank-you," she said.

"You're welcome," he replied, still a tad too nervous to hug her back.

- 7 -

"Happy Fourth of July!" Roger Riggs greeted—the mayor of Hallowed Hills—from atop a small podium located in the center of the town square.

The crowd of townspeople situated before the podium all applauded and cheered. Standing beside his mom and dad, wearing blue shorts and a red and white sleeveless shirt, Logan clapped his hands together. Seated in a red wagon next to him was Kaitlyn, dressed in a white jumper with an American flag on it. She was now five years old, but her height was well below average for a girl her age. Still, for the past two years she did grow in terms of her speech patterns, having finally advanced past slow verses of baby talk. She was now able to call her brother *Logan* instead of *Wo-gan*.

"My fellow Hallowed Hill-toppers," Mayor Riggs continued, "our great town has come so far. I can still remember back when I was a child and the Fourth of July felt like almost any other day. Now, as I bask in the glow of so many warm faces on this beautiful summer day, I can honestly say there is no better time to celebrate as one big family!"

The townspeople again voiced their joyful approval.

"And speaking of family," the mayor went on, "I'm proud to inform you all that as a special treat for all the children today, my son, Melvin the Magnificent, is here to perform a bunch of amazing magical tricks!"

A slightly chubby young man, dressed in a long black coat and a huge top hat, stood up before the podium and waved to the clapping crowd.

"Okay, my friends," the mayor said, "we have a ton of burgers, hot dogs, and wings on the grills. So grab yourselves a plate and have a wonderful Fourth!"

Mayor Riggs stepped down from the podium amidst another happy ovation, and Melvin the Magnificent shot a burst of brightly colored confetti from a magic wand up in the air behind his father.

"Wow!" Logan exclaimed. "That was cool!"

"Yes, it was," Dad agreed. "Now why don't we grab some cold drinks and a picnic table?"

"Hungry!" Kaitlyn shouted.

Logan immediately shot a concerned glance down at the red wagon. For the past two years, Kaitlyn's appetite had also grown larger and he had become quite accustomed to finding his little sister food. He knew exactly what it meant when she uttered that one special word formerly pronounced as *hun-gy.*

"Okay, honey," Mom smiled at her. "Mommy will get your jar of baby food."

"I don't think she wants baby food," Logan said.

"Oh, really?" Dad said. "Since when did you become an expert on all things Kaitlyn?"

He gave Logan a hearty pat on the head and mussed up his hair a bit.

"Let's go, Logan," Dad said. "Wheel your sister over to the picnic tables."

Logan picked up the handle to the wagon and began pulling Kaitlyn toward the tables and the food. He glanced back to see her excited face becoming more and more pink.

"Oh, no," he said to himself and picked up his pace.

Logan hit the brakes before the first open picnic table and looked back at his parents.

"Dad!" he called. "I got the table! Go get the food!"

"Okay!" Dad yelled back. "What do you want?"

"Burgers! Lots and lots of burgers!"

As his dad went off to the barbecue grills, his mom walked up to the picnic table and sat down beside Kaitlyn. She took out a small jar of baby food for toddlers and unscrewed the lid.

"Here are some carrots," she said and shoveled a chunky orange spoonful into Kaitlyn's mouth.

Kaitlyn swallowed the mush, but made a dissatisfied, scrunched-up face. Her mother's hand was soon back in front of her mouth, offering another orange helping. Logan watched as Kaitlyn's partially glowing eyes looked past the spoon toward her mother's fleshy wrist.

"No!" he yelled and yanked his mom's hand away, causing her to drop the spoon.

"Logan!" his mom hollered as little bits of orange splattered everywhere.

"I'm sorry! I thought she was going to eat y..."

Logan was having trouble deciding which was scarier: the glow in Kaitlyn's eyes or the rage in his mother's.

"I'm sorry," he could only repeat.

"Hey, what happened?" Dad asked, arriving on the scene with two plates of burgers.

"Oh, nothing," Mom said, grabbing a napkin. "Your son just decided to spill Kaitlyn's food all over me."

"Logan, why would you do that?" Dad asked.

"Hungry!" Kaitlyn shouted.

"Just a second, honey," Mom replied, wiping some orange off her shorts.

"Let me help you with that," Dad said, placing the plates down on the table.

As his parents concentrated on cleaning up the mess, Logan glanced over at his little sister. She was on the verge of turning purple and her eyes had already changed to green. Logan quickly pulled over a plate of burgers and ripped off a small piece of pinkish meat. After making sure that his parents were still focused on his mom's stained clothes, he tossed the meat across the table at Kaitlyn. She caught it in her mouth like a trained seal.

"Yes," Logan whispered.

Kaitlyn ground up the beef in an instant and swallowed.

"Hungry!" she said, pointing at her wide-open mouth.

"All right, Kaitlyn," Mom said, "I'm almost finished."

Seeing that his mother was almost through with cleaning up her mess, Logan looked to buy some extra time.

"Uh, Mom, where does meat come from?" he asked, slyly picking at the burger.

"Cows, Logan," Mom answered quickly, concentrating more on removing the stain.

Logan rapidly ripped off a much larger chunk of burger and completed another forward pass to his sister's gaping mouth. Kaitlyn finished the air-mailed meat as a much lighter pink pigment flushed over her face just as Mom turned back to her.

"Okay, honey," she said, holding the jar of baby food. "Now you can have some more."

"I no hungry," Kaitlyn grinned.

- 8 -

With the barbeque drawing to a close and the night sky growing dark, a large group of eager children surrounded a stage in the center of the town square. Logan sat with Kaitlyn on one side and Joe on the other. Mayor Riggs stood before a microphone with a large smile. Logan leaned over to Joe and whispered, "Thanks again for not telling your mom that Kaitlyn tried to eat you that time."

"It's okay," Joe replied. "She was too little to know better."

"Oh, yeah. She was."

Logan looked down at the ground, but caught Kaitlyn out of the corner of his eye. She appeared to be sitting quietly, skin completely normal. He was a bit surprised at her calmness, but appreciated it nonetheless.

"Ladies and gentlemen!" Mayor Riggs called out with the microphone. "Prepare to be amazed and mystified! I present to you, Melvin the Magnificent!"

A huge puff of smoke erupted from just beyond the podium. Ooo's and ahh's emanated from the young ones seated in the front row. The smoke cleared, revealing Melvin, dressed in his magician's jacket and large top hat. He shot his hands up in the air, releasing a white bird from both his palms. The crowd loved it.

"Wow, cool," Logan smiled.

"Happy Fourth of July, everyone!" Melvin shouted. "Let's see some magic!"

The crowd clapped their approval as Melvin got his act under way. The show was incredible. Melvin was indeed a masterful magician, making decks of cards dance on the ground, shooting small balls of fire from his magic wand, and pulling rabbits out of his sleeves instead of his hat! The audience became more enthralled with each illusion.

At one point, Melvin stepped up right before the front row of children. He whipped out his magic wand and began scanning through the long line of young faces. His gaze stopped on Kaitlyn. He stepped up before her.

"Hello, little lady," he said.

Kaitlyn smiled.

Melvin held out his wand to her and began shaking it around and around. He chanted, "Candy is sweet and lemons are sour, don't smell my feet, instead smell a flower!"

Melvin thrust his wand downward. There was a loud *snap*. The audience gasped. Kaitlyn covered her eyes. Even Logan and Joe jerked back.

"Take a look, my dear," Melvin whispered.

Kaitlyn lowered her hands to see that the magician was now holding a long-stemmed rose. The crowd again began clapping. Melvin held the rose out to Kaitlyn.

"Go ahead, take it," he said.

Kaitlyn reached out and wrapped her tiny fingers around the stem of the rose. Melvin released his grip on the flower and applauded his small assistant. The crowd did the same. Kaitlyn gazed deeply down at the red petals and raised the stem closer to her face.

"Thank you very much," Melvin addressed the cheering masses.

The joyful ovation gradually turned to laughter and short gasps. Confused, Melvin looked down to see that Kaitlyn had taken a huge bite out of the rose.

"Kaitlyn!" Logan exclaimed. "Don't eat that."

After getting a good taste of the flower, she agreed with her brother and released a small waterfall of red petals down her chin. The surrounding adults and kids could not contain their chuckles. Logan could even hear a couple of rude comments being uttered. Kaitlyn simply sat quietly, as if nothing strange had happened.

"My friends, please don't laugh at this sweet child's innocence," Melvin pleaded to the masses and then cast his eyes down at Kaitlyn. "Don't worry, my dear. You can eat that flower if you like."

- 9 -

Logan tossed and turned in his bed. It was the night before his first day of school and thoughts of what perils lay in store with the third grade refused to escape his mind. He always felt nervous before starting a new school year, but this year had some extra-crazy going for it: Kaitlyn would now be going to school with him!

"Now, be sure to look after your sister at school to-morrow," Mom had said before she tucked Logan in that night.

"Mom, why do I always have to be the one watching over Kaitlyn," he asked her.

"Because, Logan, you're her big brother and it's your special job to make sure that she's taken care of. That's what big brothers do. When I was little, my big brother took very good care of me and I grew up very happy because of it. Can you do the same for Kaitlyn?"

If only she knew how seriously Logan took that request. In fact, he had been carefully *looking after* Kaitlyn for the past couple of years. It was not an easy decision for him to make. He'd definitely worn pee-wee football helmet and pads during all the initial *test feedings* with his sister. Fortunately, after some successful trial runs, he developed a trust toward her.

From that point on, any time that Kaitlyn's skin changed color, he was there with some form of meat. Whenever she showed her sharp teeth around one of his friends, he directed her toward the refrigerator. And when she got up in the middle of the night with a growling belly, he always snagged her a snack. Logan actually began keeping a cooler of meat hidden in his closet in order to save a trip all the way downstairs.

Now, though, all means of *Kaitlyn control* had to be brought up to a whole new level. They weren't confined merely to their house. Kaitlyn was going to be set loose in much larger surroundings and Logan had no idea how he'd be able to keep an eye on her. His thoughts had grown so heavy that his eyelids could no longer remain open. He took one last glance at his cowboy clock, which was reading 10:45, and then finally entered dreamland.

A loud thump woke him up. He looked over at the cowboy clock. It was now midnight. An unexpected breeze went circling past the bed. He scanned his bedroom and saw that one of his windows was open. He hopped out of bed and nearly tripped over the opened cooler on the floor.

"Whoa!" Logan exclaimed, catching his balance.

He picked up the cooler and peered inside. It was empty.

"She ate all the meat," he gasped and then turned his gaze toward the open window. "Now, where is she? She didn't…"

He rushed up to the windowsill just in time to see a small shadow with long hair scurrying down the street.

"Kaitlyn!" he shouted, but then slapped his hand over his mouth.

He didn't want to risk waking up his parents. He quickly put on his slippers and climbed up on the windowsill. The second floor of his house was not very far off the ground, and there was an overhang on the first floor he could jump onto. Logan could tell that Kaitlyn had landed on the large bush directly below from the small indentation on top of the shrubbery.

Without giving a second thought to it, he slid out of the window and began climbing. Two seconds later, his backside was surrounded by twigs and soft tiny green leaves. He hopped out of the bush and headed in the

direction of Kaitlyn's shadow. Only her shadow was now nowhere in sight.

She's far ahead! Logan thought. *I have to hurry!*

He darted down the quiet road, hoping to pick up on his sister's trail.

Meanwhile, about two blocks away, Kaitlyn moved with lightning-quick precision toward a nearby field. Her bright green eyes could be seen in the night, like two small safety reflectors that colorfully illuminated her fully purple skin.

She turned off the road and disappeared into the field's long blades of grass. Her nostrils flared as if a tasty scent was in the air. A small farm lay off in the distance. The tall grass blades rustled back and forth, as she approached closer and closer.

A few cows were quietly grazing in a pasture enclosed by an old wooden fence beside a red, two-story barn. A brick farmhouse sat about thirty yards behind the pasture.

"Moooo!" went two white and black-splotched cows as they chewed on the grass before them.

One particular cow with a pink, spotted nose rested on the ground, eyes half closed. Kaitlyn abruptly popped up behind it and slapped her hands down on its black and white back. The cow's eyes sprung open into two large black discs.

"Hungry!" Kaitlyn grinned.

She opened her sharp-tooth mouth and plunged her face down into the cow.

Back at the edge of the field, Logan heard the cow screaming out a very loud, painful, "Moo."

She's at Mr. Crabtree's farm! he thought and dashed into the field of tall grass.

The cow's cries became more thunderous with every step that Logan took. Upon coming out of the field, he instantly spotted his sister hovering over the writhing cow.

"Kaitlyn!" he shouted without stopping his hustling slippers.

She looked up from her *snack* with blood dripping down the sides of her mouth. She saw Logan and smiled, her eyes and skin returning to normal.

"Logan," she said and waved at her brother.

Logan came rushing over and pulled her off the cow, holding her tightly.

"Kaitlyn, what are you doing?" he asked. "This is very bad! No eating cows!"

"I was hungry," she repeated. "It's meat! Mom said!"

Suddenly, a light was turned on in the window of the farmhouse. The front door began opening.

"Oh no!" Logan said. "It's Farmer Crabtree! Come on, Kaitlyn, we have to go right now!"

He lowered his sister's bare feet to the ground and held tightly onto her hand. He pumped his legs into motion and the two sped off back toward the field.

"Who's out there?" Farmer Crabtree hollered as he hurried out of his house in a robe, holding a pitchfork. "I'll stick ya good!"

Breathing heavily, Logan could hear the farmer's footsteps charging out to the pasture. Keeping a tight grip on Kaitlyn's hand, he charged into the tall blades of grass. The farmer's stomping feet were getting closer. Logan at once ducked down low to the ground, pulling his sister with him.

"Why did we fall?" Kaitlyn asked.

"Shhh," he whispered. "He'll hear us."

The grass blades a couple of feet away from them made crunching sounds as Farmer Crabtree came striding forward.

"Okay, where are ya!" he shouted. "There's no use hiding! I ain't putting up with you pesky kids anymore!"

Logan gently placed his hand over Kaitlyn's bloody mouth just in case she felt like answering the farmer back.

"You kids are in big trouble!" Farmer Crabtree yelled and violently shoved his pitchfork down into the grass.

He lifted up his weapon and brought its sharp points down into another section of the ground. Logan pulled

Kaitlyn closer, hoping to avoid the pitchfork's sharp sting. Farmer Crabtree raised the metal points directly over them. Logan closed his eyes in terror. Suddenly, one of the cows back in the pasture let out a blood-curdling *Moo*. The farmer turned toward the barn, shifting the direction of the pitchfork.

"Ah, shoot," he muttered and looked out at the stretch of empty grass. "You're lucky my cow needs me! I better never see you kids around here again!"

Farmer Crabtree walked back to the pasture. Once Logan no longer heard his footsteps, he retook Kaitlyn's hand and led her out of the field without looking back.

Back at the pasture, Farmer Crabtree ran up to his injured cow, which was still lying on the ground. He gazed down at the fallen bovine.

"What in the world?" he said, noticing the bite marks amidst the black and white skin. "Must have been a baby coyote or something."

- 10 -

Logan nervously tapped a pencil on his desk in Mrs. Brissano's 3rd grade classroom. Though he should have been writing down his teacher's instructions, he couldn't keep his mind from wondering what was happening with Kaitlyn in her own classroom down the hall. Before dropping her off, he made sure to give her a few extra pieces of meat to hopefully keep her tummy satisfied until lunch. He also had her put on her glasses because of the partially tinted lenses that somewhat concealed her eyes whenever they began to show shades of green.

Fortunately, Kaitlyn was also paired up with a teacher's aid, who would be working with her throughout the school day.

Mom explained to Logan that some of the school's officials thought that Kaitlyn might be a slow learner and would thus need to be assigned someone to help her keep up with the rest of the kids in her class.

Logan didn't quite understand the reasoning because Kaitlyn had never seemed slow to him, but at least he felt good knowing an adult would be keeping an eye specifically on her.

Meanwhile, four doors down the hall, a large group of kindergarteners were seated on a huge square rug before their teacher, Mrs. Mahoney.

She had two puppets on her hand, a dragon and a princess, and was performing a show.

"Now I'm going to eat you for lunch, Princess," Mrs. Mahoney made the dragon puppet talk in a low voice.

The children smiled and laughed. Kaitlyn kept her mouth closed and stared at the dragon. Her young teacher's aid, Karen, sat beside her.

"No, please, Dragon, don't eat me." Mrs. Mahoney made the princess speak in a sweet, high voice. "We're in kindergarten now, and you don't act like that here."

"Stop with your talking," the dragon roared. "It's lunch time!"

"Not today, Dragon. You haven't met Miss Hammy yet!"

"Who's that?"

Mrs. Mahoney turned her back to the audience. She soon spun back around holding a small glass tank in her princess puppet hand.

Behind the clear glass walls sat a live guinea pig with white and brown fur. The students gasped with delight and laughed. Kaitlyn's eyes widened.

"Miss Hammy is the kindergarten's class pet," the princess said. "She protects me and everyone else from all mean dragons."

"Oh no!" cried the dragon. "I'm sorry! I'll be nice!"

The children all cheered. Mrs. Mahoney and the princess held out Miss Hammy's cage to the happy audience. Kaitlyn stood up and reached out for the tank.

"Hungry!" she shouted.

Mrs. Mahoney pulled back the cage.

"No, Kaitlyn," she said. "It's Hammy, Miss Hammy."

The children all began laughing at Kaitlyn's outburst. Karen stood up and gently touched Kaitlyn's outstretched hand.

"It's okay, Kaitlyn," she said. "We need to stay seated during the puppet show. Would you like a snack?"

Kaitlyn nodded her head.

"All right, let's go to the snack table," Karen said and took her hand.

Kaitlyn pointed at Miss Hammy as the aid led her off the carpet. The rest of the class continued their chuckling.

"Thank you, Karen," Mrs. Mahoney said and looked down at the students. "Children, please calm down."

- 11 -

Logan took a big bite of his peanut butter and jelly sandwich in the school cafeteria. Worrying about Kaitlyn during the entire first half of the first day of school had made him very hungry.

"Is this the first time you ate anything today?" Joe asked.

Logan took a big guzzle of his carton of chocolate milk before answering, "No, I'm just really hungry. I can't explain why."

"It must be one good PB & J."

"Maybe it is."

A loud shriek suddenly erupted from the back of the cafeteria. Logan dropped his sandwich to the table.

"What was that?" Joe asked.

"Look!" shouted another student.

Logan shot a glance toward the back of the cafeteria to see Kaitlyn running out of the kitchen with a piece of pepperoni pizza dangling from her mouth. Wrinkly Lunch Lady Diana, with her reddish hair tied up in a hairnet and wearing plastic serving gloves, rushed after her, swinging a soup ladle.

"Come back here!" the lunch lady cackled.

"Oh, no," Logan frowned.

The entire cafeteria immediately focused on Kaitlyn. Rows of laughter rose up as she scampered across the floor.

"Logan, that's your sister!" Joe said.

"I know," Logan groaned and got up out of his seat.

Kaitlyn had already sucked up half the slice of pizza as Lunch Lady Diana caught up to her.

"Stop!" the lunch lady bellowed and pounced forward. "Gotcha!"

At the last second, Kaitlyn jumped onto a long row of connected lunch tables, nearly escaping Diana's plastic-gloved grasp.

She scuttled across an array of sandwiches and juice boxes as the lunch lady landed on her face. An uproar of childish laughter filled the cafeteria. Amidst all the hilarity, Logan took a shortcut through the second row of lunch tables, hoping to meet up with his sister.

"Get back here!" Lunch Lady Diana hollered, picking herself off the floor.

With just the crust of the pizza left protruding from her mouth, Kaitlyn hurried toward the end of the long stretch of tables, knocking a carton of milk onto the floor. She jumped off the edge and was instantly caught in Logan's arms.

Her rough impact sent him straight to the floor. Lunch Lady Diana rushed up before them.

"You're in big trouble, misseeeeeee!" she shrieked as her feet slipped on the recently spilled milk.

The lunch lady landed with a huge thud on her backside, right next to Logan and Kaitlyn. The laughing in the cafeteria reached a brand new level of loudness. Logan's face turned red as he looked at his sister's pink, angelic visage.

"Kaitlyn, why did you do that?" he asked.

"Logan," she smiled. "I was hungry."

A crumpled-up piece of tin foil suddenly hit Logan in the face. He glanced up in the direction of the assault to see Paul, a fifth grader and resident school bully, pointing at him.

"Your sister's a freak," Paul taunted. "Just like you!"

Logan silently looked away and closed his eyes. The non-stop snickering of his fellow classmates filled his ears and was soon replaced by the grumbling of Kaitlyn's still-not-satisfied belly.

That was when he reached the scary realization that he would never be able to always keep track of her.

- 12 -

The walk home from the first day of school felt more like a walk of shame for Logan. He kept his eye on Kaitlyn as she skipped down the sidewalk a couple of paces ahead of him and Joe.

"You think she enjoyed her first day of school?" Joe asked, nodding at Kaitlyn.

"Ha ha," Logan pretended to laugh. "This was probably one of the worst days of my life. And it's all because of her. Some kids were calling us *brother and sister freak*. She ruined everything."

"I'm sorry. Hey, maybe it won't be so bad. She's just your sister and she's only in kindergarten."

"I can't watch her forever. It's impossible."

"Watch her forever? You don't have to? The aid has to watch over her."

"It's just different than that, Joe. She's different. She's..."

The gruff barking of a dog interrupted Logan. Kaitlyn stopped in her tracks and stared at the front lawn adjacent to the sidewalk. A small black and white pug, tied to the porch of a cape-style house, was yapping away at Kaitlyn. Logan and Joe soon caught up to the motionless Kaitlyn.

"What is it, Kaitlyn?" Logan asked.

"It's a doggie," Kaitlyn replied, pointing her finger at the porch. "Is he hungry?"

"That's Rocky. He's a good dog, but I don't know if he's hungry. Besides, we don't have any doggie food. Come on, let's go."

Logan and Joe began walking ahead. Kaitlyn remained still. The pug continued its non-stop barking spree.

"Kaitlyn!" Logan called. "Come on! It's time to go home!"

His words broke Kaitlyn from her frozen state. She turned away from the pug and hustled up after her big brother.

"See what I mean, Joe?" Logan said. "It's never easy."

"Come on, Logan," Joe said. "Think happy thoughts. Like my birthday party this weekend. It's gonna be so cool. My parents even hired Melvin the Magnificent to do a bunch of tricks."

"Really? That is cool. Plus, my parents will be there so I won't have to keep watch over Kaitlyn."

"Wow, man. You talk about her like she's some special assignment. She's only a kindergartener."

Logan looked down at the sidewalk and slightly shook his head.

"Yeah, Joe, you're right," he lied.

- 13 -

Children screamed and ran around like untamed animals in party hats in the backyard of Joe's home. Logan was happy to join in with the herd as Kaitlyn bounced happily up and down on her mother's lap. Joe's father stood behind a large barbecue grill, unwrapping raw burgers and hot dogs.

"This is a great party!" Logan said to Joe as the two passed a Nerf football back and forth with their friend, Jeff.

"Oh, yes!" Joe agreed. "And did you see all the presents? Maybe you can stay here after the party and we can play with all my new toys!"

"That would be awesome!"

"I want to stay, too!" Jeff shouted. "But, Logan, don't let your lame sister stay. She's a weirdo."

At the large gas grill, Joe's father lit up the burners. A steady stream of controlled fire ignited across the base. He lowered the lid to find Kaitlyn staring up at him with a paper plate in her hands.

"Hungry," she said.

"Hi, Kaitlyn," Joe's father said. "The burgers and hot dogs will be ready soon, but first, the magician is going to perform some tricks for everyone. You want to see that, don't you?"

"Hungry!" Kaitlyn replied.

Joe's father laughed heartily and walked out from behind the grill. He patted Kaitlyn on the head.

"Don't worry, sweetie," he said. "The food will be ready right after the magic show. Now, come over and sit with the rest of the kids. The show's about to start."

"Honey!" called Joe's mother, standing next to a small, portable stage. "Come get the video camera!"

"Coming!" Joe's father yelled back and jogged off toward her.

Kaitlyn remained next to the grill.

Seated front and center before the stage, Logan and Joe waited excitedly for the start of the show.

"This is so cool," Logan smiled. "I can't believe your parents got Melvin the Magnificent for your party."

"I know," Joe answered. "My dad is friends with Mayor Riggs."

Joe's mother stepped up before the audience of children and parents.

"Ladies, gentlemen, and children," she said, "we're so happy to have you all here at Joe's birthday party. Thank you for coming. Now, without any further ado, I present to you all, Melvin the Magnificent!"

She quickly walked out of the way as the stage began emitting a soft haze of smoke. Suddenly, a large black top hat appeared out of nowhere. It began dancing back and forth in mid-air. The display had all the children and adults either smiling or laughing.

The jumping hat abruptly shot up very high, then came falling back down and immediately stopped six feet above the smoky stage. As the puffy haze began to clear, the shape of a body emerged beneath the hat.

"I see him!" one of the children shouted.

Soon, Melvin the Magnificent—dressed in his signature long black coat—stepped forth to the edge of the stage. The crowd cheered. Melvin held the brim of his top hat and gestured a warm smile.

"Thank you everyone," Melvin said. "Welcome to the party! And welcome to the show!"

Everyone clapped.

"My hat has been acting up a little lately," he continued. "I do hope that nothing is wrong."

Suddenly, Melvin's top hat started to magically move upwards. The children began to laugh. Before the hat left his head, he grabbed onto its brim with both hands and pulled it back down.

"Pesky hat," he said. "Now, I believe there's a birthday boy in the audience. Joe, please stand up."

Joe jumped to his feet and the crowd clapped for him.

"Ah, yes," Melvin grinned and stepped off the stage. "Would you mind holding out your hand, Joe?"

Joe rapidly extended his arm, palm up. Melvin reached out his empty hand and snapped his fingers. A small, rectangular card appeared amidst a tiny puff of smoke between his thumb and index finger.

"Happy birthday, Joe," Melvin smiled. "This card entitles you to a free magic trick at my shop."

Melvin handed the card over to Joe. The audience clapped. Melvin stepped back to the center of the stage.

"And, now, let the show begin!" he shouted.

The children and parents all cheered him on. A magic wand shot out of Melvin's sleeve. He raised it up to the sky. A loud crash immediately followed and some small, circular pieces of charcoal spilled onto the stage. Everyone's eyes shot toward the source of the crash to find that the grill had been knocked over... and Kaitlyn was standing right next to it. She held a packet of raw hamburger meat in her hands.

"What's she doing?" asked a random parent in the crowd.

"Kaitlyn!" Logan's mom exclaimed.

Suddenly, the edge of the stage supporting the spilled grill burst into flames. Everyone in the backyard began screaming and running away. Even Melvin the Magnificent hopped off the stage and jogged toward the house.

"It's okay, kids," he tried to say calmly. "It's just a little accident."

Joe's father quickly ran to the grill and dumped a large bottle of soda on it. The flames began to die down, and another adult promptly rushed up to the stage and dumped some more liquid refreshment on it.

As the roaring flames were extinguished, Logan could hear the dialogue gradually coming forth from the crowd.

"What's the matter with that girl?"

"She could have hurt someone."

"Why is she holding that pack of raw meat?"

The statements were too much for Logan to handle. He closed his eyes and covered his ears as his father ran up to Kaitlyn and picked her up. As she was carried away from the grill, Kaitlyn looked out at the group of parents scolding her and children laughing at her. She gently lowered her head onto her father's shoulder.

"Logan, your sister is so weird," Jeff said, patting him on the back. "What's the matter with her? She really is some sort of stupid freak."

Logan looked at Jeff and shook his head.

"I didn't..."

"Logan!" Joe shouted angrily. "Your sister ruined my birthday party!"

- 14 -

A brisk, autumn wind blew through the trees on Monday morning. With his head lowered, Logan walked slowly to school.

Kaitlyn scampered a few paces ahead of him. She made it to the edge of the crosswalk and stopped.

She looked back at Logan and jogged over to him.

"Do you have food for me, Logan?" she asked, pointing to her mouth.

"No, Kaitlyn," Logan frowned. "I didn't feed you yesterday, and I'm not feeding you today. I'm through keeping track of you and your food."

"But I'm hungry."

"I don't care anymore. You're ruining my life. Don't you get it? The kids at school think I'm a freak and now Joe doesn't even want to talk to me."

Kaitlyn stared quietly at her brother.

"It's all because of you!" Logan yelled and walked off toward the crosswalk.

He took one step onto the road and halted. He glanced back at Kaitlyn. Her gaze and feet remained frozen.

"Let's go," he said, waving her over. "I still have to walk you to school."

Kaitlyn hurried up beside him. Logan grudgingly took her hand and led her across the street.

While walking through the schoolyard, Logan could hear some kids shouting statements of torment.

"Hey, look! It's the freak twins!"

"Who's got a slice of pizza?"

"Maybe some raw hamburger!"

Logan tightly closed his eyes and released his grip on Kaitlyn's hand. He hurried inside the school without looking back at her, but listened to be sure she was still behind him. After dropping Kaitlyn off with Karen, her aid, Logan entered his third grade classroom and sat down at his desk.

Most of the students were already seated, but Mrs. Brissano hadn't arrived yet.

Logan looked over at Joe, who was in the row next to his. "Joe," he whispered. "Where's Mrs. Brissano?"

Joe turned his head slightly and merely shrugged his shoulders. Without saying a word, he looked away.

Before Logan could attempt another apology for Kaitlyn's blazing birthday blow-up, the classroom door swung open.

Every student looked toward the front of the room as Mrs. Brissano rushed in, closing the door behind her.

"Excuse me, children," the teacher said. "I have some very serious news that I need to discuss with you."

The students were silent.

"The principal feels that it's best for each teacher to discuss this with their class with the hope of finding some answers," Mrs. Brissano said. "As of last night, Jeff Webber has been reported missing by his parents."

The classroom let out short gasps of fright. Logan immediately looked over at the empty desk near the front of the room where Jeff usually sat.

He'd just seen him at Joe's party over the weekend. An eerie chill ran up his spine.

- 15 -

With a tray in hand, Logan slowly moved along the lunch line in the cafeteria. Because of the morning's negative news and events, he wasn't feeling very hungry. He kept thinking about Jeff and what could have possibly happened to him.

"Hey, kid!" Lunch Lady Diana called out. "You hungry or not?"

Logan merely stared down at his tray resting on the metal food platform.

"Hey!" Lunch Lady Diana repeated.

Logan abruptly felt a harsh slap to the back of his head. He snapped out of his pondering state and spun around to see Paul grinning at him.

"You're totally lost, just like Jeff," the bully snarled.

Embarrassed, Logan frowned and turned away from the much larger Paul. He felt bad upon hearing Jeff's name again.

"Are... you... hungry?" Lunch Lady Diana loudly uttered.

All Logan heard was *hungry* as his mind continued picturing Jeff's face. Suddenly, an ominous idea entered his head.

I stopped feeding Kaitlyn yesterday, he thought. *And Jeff disappeared yesterday. She couldn't have... would she eat... no way... but...*

He picked up his tray and exited the lunch line.

"Hey!" Lunch Lady Diana called. "Where are you going?"

"I'm not hungry!" Logan shouted back.

- 16 -

At 2:58 p.m., Logan waited impatiently outside the door to the kindergarten classroom. He was in a rush to get home and quickly put all of the day's bothersome events behind him.

A loud ruckus erupted inside the classroom, which caused his ears to perk up. He ran up to the door's rectangular window and peered inside.

Kaitlyn was chasing a small group of screaming children around the room. Her skin was turning pink. Karen was attempting to break up the commotion. With a grumpy huff, Logan opened up the door and quickly entered the classroom.

"Kaitlyn!" he shouted.

Kaitlyn's pattering feet immediately ceased movement. The screaming children ran off to the safety of their coat cubbies. Logan marched up to his little sister.

"We're going home," he said sternly and grabbed her hand.

Though she was fairly wound up, she allowed him to lead her away from the class. Neither Karen nor Mrs. Mahoney could say anything further, choosing to focus on getting the rest of the children packed up for the day.

Outside the school, Logan hurried Kaitlyn across the street. Once they reached the sidewalk, he breathed a little bit easier.

"Good, we're far enough away," he said, looking back at the now distant school.

Logan slowed his footsteps a bit and let go of Kaitlyn's hand.

"What were you doing back there?" he asked, angry. "Why do you have to act so crazy?"

"I was hungry, Logan," Kaitlyn simply replied.

"Well, you're going to have to start learning to be patient and control yourself when you feel hungry. Why can't you just..."

The shrill screeching of tires stopped Logan's speech. The noise was abruptly followed by a thud and a high-pitched yelp. Logan looked up the street to see a black jeep positioned awkwardly on a slight angle in the center of the road.

"What happened?" he asked.

Logan glanced back down at Kaitlyn to learn that she had sped further away from him toward the jeep.

"Hey, get back here!" he called out. "What are you doing?"

Kaitlyn did not turn around and kept moving faster.

"Wait!" Logan shouted and darted after her.

The owner of the black jeep, a young man wearing a backwards baseball cap, stepped out onto the road. Kaitlyn rushed past and actually startled him.

"Oh, honey, is he yours?" he said apologetically.

Kaitlyn silently ducked behind the front bumper of the jeep as Logan finally arrived on the scene.

"Kaitlyn?" Logan called.

"I'm so sorry," the jeep owner said. "Is that her dog?"

"What?" Logan asked and stepped toward the front of the jeep.

He found Kaitlyn on her knees with her back turned to him.

"Kaitlyn," he said. "What is it?"

His little sister remained silent, her head briefly bouncing up and down. Logan slowly walked forward, extending his hand to offer her a consoling pat on the back. Upon coming into contact with her face, he sharply pulled back his hand.

"Kaitlyn!" Logan said in shock. "What are you doing?"

She was unable to reply with the pug—Rocky—dangling from her mouth. She was trying to eat the puppy.

"Get that dead dog out of your mouth right now!" Logan exclaimed. "Why would you do that? Spit it out, now!"

After a few more bites, Kaitlyn opened her mouth, dropping Rocky back onto the street.

"Whoa," said the jeep's owner. "This is all too weird."

"Kaitlyn, get away from the dog!" Logan shouted.

"No, Logan," Kaitlyn said, pointing down at Rocky. "The doggie's not dead."

Logan gazed down at Rocky's motionless body. Suddenly, the dog's eyes popped open.

"Whoa!" Logan and the jeep's owner both said, jumping back.

Kaitlyn remained kneeling. Rocky emitted a soft cry. His eyes began to glow green. His snout curled into a snarl, revealing his sharp, white teeth. Logan reached down and yanked Kaitlyn off the road.

"Get away from it!" he yelled.

Rocky leapt into the air like an acrobat. The second his paws touched down on the road, he flashed a wild, green-eyed, big-toothed grin.

"I'm out of here!" the jeep's owner exclaimed and ducked back into his vehicle.

"Come on, Kaitlyn!" Logan said, dragging her over to the sidewalk. "Let's get out of here!"

"Why?" Kaitlyn asked as she helplessly hung on to her big brother's frantic grip.

"Because you're not the only one who's hungry!"

The two reached the sidewalk in half a second and immediately went bounding down it. Rocky wasted no time charging after them, his open mouth leaving a trail of salivating drool.

"Run fast, Kaitlyn!" Logan yelled, grasping her hand tightly.

Kaitlyn kept her mouth shut and did as her brother said. Her profusely pumping legs had no trouble keeping up with him. Rocky listened to Logan as well, refusing to let up his relentless speed.

Rocky chased them down the sidewalk, through a set of bushes, and onto their street. Logan clutched his free hand around his house key in his jacket pocket and glanced over his shoulder. Rocky was still on their tail and didn't appear to be getting tired.

"Okay, Kaitlyn, there's our house," Logan exhaled between breaths. "We've got to make it inside before Rocky gets us."

Kaitlyn didn't reply, choosing to continue her little legs' brisk motions. The two raced up their front lawn as Logan took out his house key. Rocky rapidly reached the lawn as well, about to close in.

"Get ready!" he shouted to Kaitlyn.

Logan jammed the key into the front door's lock and twisted it clockwise. After a little *click*, the door gave way. Rocky jumped right at them. Without looking back, Logan dragged Kaitlyn inside and slammed the door closed behind them. He sat down with his back to the door and breathed out a sigh of relief.

"We're home," he said, closing his eyes. "We're safe."

As Logan continued breathing heavy, Kaitlyn grinned and covered her mouth. Tiny bursts of laughter leaked out from the edges of her muffling hand. With a confused expression, Logan glanced over at his sister.

"The doggie still made it in," she smiled.

"Huh?" Logan raised an eyebrow.

An abrupt *huff* was emitted from his far right side. Logan slowly turned toward the sound to find Rocky standing eagerly on all fours. The small dog's eyes shone like two bright green beams. His hind legs were poised like tightly-wound springs.

"No way," Logan grunted under his breath, unable to move.

"Doggie!" Kaitlyn shouted, pointing her finger.

Rocky at once burst forward at full speed. He jumped up in the air, his mouth wide open. Logan's reflexes finally overcame his fear and forced him to duck back out of the way. Rocky crashed face-first into the door and flopped onto the floor.

"Run, Kaitlyn!" Logan yelled, sprinting away from the front door.

Rocky stood back up and vibrantly shook his head from side to side. He immediately picked up on Logan's pounding footsteps and took off after him. Once the two were away from the area inside the front door, Kaitlyn trotted into the kitchen.

As Logan darted through the living room, he frantically attempted to think of some way to get himself and Kaitlyn out of their current situation. Rocky appeared to care very little about Logan's thought process as he barked madly during the pursuit.

"Rocky, stop it!" Logan pointlessly pleaded with the pup.

He grabbed the wireless controller to his video game system and flung it backwards. Rocky caught the controller in his mouth, realized that it wasn't food, and spit it to the floor.

Logan rounded the living room and looked to head back toward the front of the house. He glanced over his shoulder to see his four-legged foe was lagging a bit behind. This was his chance to grab Kaitlyn and escape out the front door.

"Kaitl..." he began, but tripped over his video game controller.

He smacked his face into the floor, a few feet shy of the front door. Rocky soon caught up and lunged through the air. Logan looked back with only enough time to see the menacing pug flying at him.

A small arm shot into view out of nowhere and grabbed hold of Rocky before he could land. Logan's eyes opened wide in shock upon witnessing Kaitlyn dangling the puppy like a yo-yo. Rocky didn't take kindly to his capture and growled furiously.

"No, doggie!" Kaitlyn scolded him.

Rocky's yapping instantly ceased. Kaitlyn held up a small meatball in her free hand.

"Here," she said and shoved the round piece of beef into Rocky's mouth.

The puppy happily devoured the treat in seconds. The green glow in his eyes began to fade. Kaitlyn placed him on the floor and walked up to the front door.

"You go home," she said while opening the door.

As if the little girl was his master, Rocky trotted right past Logan, who was still on the floor, and exited the house.

Kaitlyn closed the door and walked up to her speechless brother. "The doggie's gone now," she smiled.

- 17 -

"Did you remember to get meat for burgers?" Logan asked his mom as they exited the supermarket at the center of town.

"Oh my goodness, I forgot!" Mom replied.

She stopped pushing the shopping cart, which contained five grocery bags, as well as Kaitlyn in the front child's seat, and glanced back at the store.

"No burgers?" Kaitlyn frowned.

Mom looked back to her daughter.

"Yes, burgers, honey," she smiled. "We just have to run back and get the meat."

"Aw, man," Logan shrugged and gazed across the street at Melvin the Magnificent's Costume/Magic Shop and Theater.

He saw Joe and his mother entering the shop.

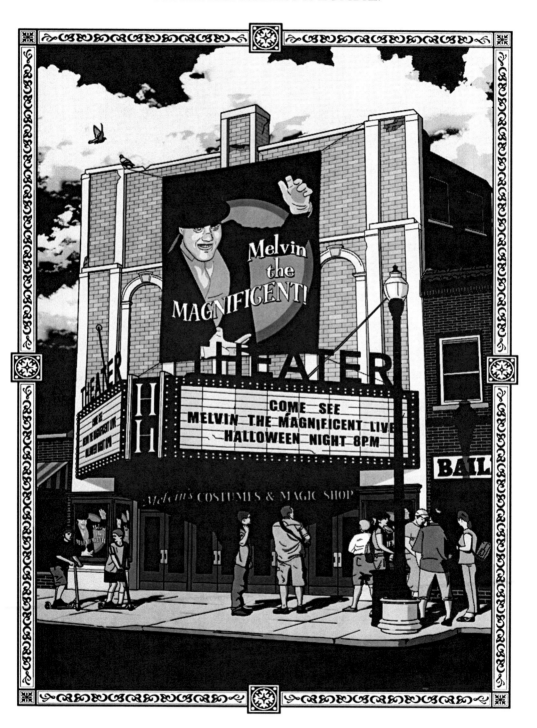

"Hey, Mom, can I go check out the magic shop while you go back in?" Logan asked. "I just saw Joe and his mom go in."

"Well, all right," Mom said. "Just don't be too long. I'll come pick you up once Kaitlyn and I are done."

"Great! Thanks!"

Logan dashed off in the direction of the magic shop.

"And stay with Joe's mother the entire time!" his mother shouted.

"Okay!" he called back.

After carefully crossing the street, Logan jogged up to the magic shop's entrance, which had a large theater marquee above it advertising Melvin the Magnificent's next show on Halloween. A string of bells jingled Logan's presence as he walked inside.

The bottom level of the two-story shop looked somewhat small from the outside, but was very deep and wide on the inside. The walls were lined with numerous magic tricks and props.

Logan could hear Joe down one particular aisle that was loaded with costumes hanging on racks. He followed Joe's voice and soon located his friend.

"Hey, Joe," Logan said, walking up to him.

Joe turned his way and half smiled.

"Hey, Logan," Joe said. "What are you doing here?"

"I saw you and your mom coming in here. I just wanted to say hi, maybe check out some of the magic tricks. Where's your mom?"

"She's just checking out the theater in the back."

Joe pointed to an open doorway with a red curtain draped around it.

"Oh yeah, remember the magic show we saw there last Christmas?" Logan asked.

A tall figure stepped up behind Logan.

"I do remember that show," bellowed a proud, showman's voice.

Logan turned around to find Melvin the Magnificent towering over him. He took a step back beside Joe. Both boys' mouths were agape in star-struck awe.

"It's Melvin the Magnificent," Joe whispered.

"Hi there, Joe," Melvin grinned. "And how are you, Logan?"

With wide eyes, Logan gingerly leaned next to Joe and softly said, "He knows our names."

Joe gave him a little nudge that silently said, "Stay calm."

"Of course, I know you two," Melvin nodded. "Welcome. Now tell me, what brings you boys to the shop today?"

Joe held out the gift card he'd received at his party.

"Ah, excellent, a gift card redemption," the magician smiled. "I hope you're finding everything okay."

Melvin cast a glance past the boys.

"Now, you two didn't come in here by yourselves, did you?" he asked. "I just heard about the missing Webber boy; just terrible."

"No. My mom's looking at the theater in the back," Joe replied.

"His mom's checking out the theater," Logan repeated.

"Ah, yes, yes, I see," Melvin said. "She really shouldn't be back there. There's a lot of heavy machinery and large pieces of lumber back there alone. I'm actually having the theater refurbished a bit right now to fit more seats. I'm hoping to put together another big performance for the entire town this Halloween."

"Yeah, we saw the sign out front," Joe nodded.

"And what a wonderful idea it is to do a Halloween show," Joe's mom said, emerging from the theater's curtained door. "The new construction in there looks great so far."

"Oh, thank you," Melvin said. "It's always great putting on a show for all the kids and their families. And my father always does such a fine job getting the word out to everyone."

"Well, your father's always been an excellent public speaker, as a good mayor should be."

"That's true. Hopefully I won't disappoint everyone on October 31st."

"I'm sure you won't. And, Logan, won't your sister be so happy to have a magic show on her birthday?"

"Oh, yeah," Logan nodded. "Great."

"Your sister was born on Halloween, right?" Melvin smiled at him. "I didn't know that till the other day when I was told. Well, I'll have to put together something special just for her. I can't believe it's almost Halloween already. I hope you find some great costumes today!"

- 18 -

The air surrounding Crabtree's Farm was filled with the merry shouts of many a youngster as families were scattered all over the place, picking pumpkins, taking pictures and going on hayrides.

The loudest of happy cries echoed forth from a large corn maze directly opposite the pumpkin patch.

"Mom, can I go there first?" Logan asked, pointing to row after row of un-husked cobs.

"Let's find some pumpkins first," his mom replied.

"Yeah, before all the good ones get picked!" his dad exclaimed, holding Kaitlyn on his shoulders.

"Punt-kins!" Kaitlyn happily hollered.

"Let's go, guys!" Dad said and jogged out toward the patch.

"Wait for us," Mom said. "Come on, Logan."

Logan took one last glance at the corn maze as his mother took his hand and dragged him toward the field of pumpkins.

"Welcome to Crabtree's Farm!" shouted a booming voice into a bullhorn. "Welcome!"

Logan turned in the direction of the voice to see Mayor Riggs, standing once again on another wooden podium before a big red barn.

"I hope you're all having a wonderful time as the frightfully fun Halloween season gets into full swing!" the mayor went on.

The group of people standing around him applauded their approval.

"I know that every year our town does a fantastic job of getting into the spirit of all things spooky," the mayor continued. "So it's with great pride that I say to you all: let the pumpkin-picking begin!"

Logan looked away as everyone cheered and clapped. His dad and Kaitlyn had already found their first prized pumpkin.

"Look at this one!" Dad shouted, holding a large pumkin over his head.

Kaitlyn was still on his shoulders and laughed with glee as the pumpkin rose up before her face.

"Go pick one for yourself, Logan," his mom said, releasing her hand from his.

Logan rushed into the patch, hoping to make a fast selection in order to be granted full access to the corn maze. After a few quick glances, he soon settled on a medium-sized pumpkin of his own.

As Dad went off to pay for their picks, Logan, his mom, and Kaitlyn went off toward the symmetrically aligned fields of corn.

"Just for a couple of minutes," Mom instructed. "Then we'll all go on the hayride."

"Okay!" Logan said and dashed ahead to the maze's entrance.

Once inside the large labyrinth of long, yellow stalks, Logan chose to navigate the path to his right. He eagerly jogged along the dirt ground, bobbing and weaving through different directions. While rounding another bend, something big popped out from the stalks, and with a shove, sent him falling to the ground.

With his face buried in the earth, he detected some childish laughter. He looked back to see Paul, his brutish older schoolmate, smirking with glee.

"Hey, freak," Paul said. "Where do you think you're going?"

Logan didn't answer. He remained seated on the ground.

"Not gonna answer me?" Paul asked. "Well, now you're in big trouble."

Logan's limbs froze with fear. Paul pounded a fist into his other hand and began walking toward Logan. Then an abrupt rustling occurred in the wall of cornstalks to the bully's right.

Logan looked in the direction of the noise just in time to see Kaitlyn come pouncing forward onto the dirt path. She landed between her brother and Paul.

Whoa!" Paul exclaimed and took a slight step back.

Kaitlyn glared a menacing, green-eyed stare at him. She opened her mouth and exhaled a hostile growl past her sharpened teeth. Paul's fist unwound as his arms dropped to his sides.

"What the..." he began.

Kaitlyn let out a louder growl and took a step toward him, reaching out her hands. Paul at once began back-pedaling away from her.

"You need to get a hold of your sister, Logan," he nervously said, still advancing in the opposite direction.

"You're a bad boy!" Kaitlyn hissed and leapt forward.

Paul immediately turned around and sprinted away. "Your whole family's crazy!" he cried out in fear.

Kaitlyn and Logan watched as Paul turned a corner and disappeared deeper into the corn maze.

Once his quickened footsteps were no longer audible, Kaitlyn looked back to her brother.

Her eyes no longer glowed green. Logan stood up and walked over to his sister.

"No more bad boy," she smiled.

Logan patted Kaitlyn on the head.

"Good girl," he said. "Thanks."

Somewhere out amongst the stalks, Paul panted heavily and continued his racing pace.

He glanced over his shoulder to see if he was being followed, but the path behind him was deserted.

Upon looking back to the front, his foot tripped over a stray vine. His chest pounded the ground and one of his sneakers fell off.

He awkwardly rose to one knee when crunching noises came from behind him.

"Who's there?" Paul tensely asked without turning around.

A large, black shadow loomed over him.

- 19 -

"When are we gonna carve these?" Dad asked as he entered their home carrying three different-sized pumpkins.

"How about we do it the day before Kaitlyn's birthday?" Mom suggested as she entered the house with her two children.

"You mean the day before Halloween?" Logan asked.

"That's right!" his mom smiled. "Now go wash up for dinner. You too, Kaitlyn."

Logan looked down at his sister.

"Come on, Kaitlyn," he said. "Let's go wash our hands."

Kaitlyn nodded and followed her brother as he went up the stairs. Upon reaching the second floor, Logan entered the bathroom and turned on the light. Kaitlyn stepped inside right behind him.

"Listen, Kaitlyn," Logan said, "I'm sorry if I was mean to you the past couple of weeks. I shouldn't have gotten so upset. I should have been giving you your *special* feedings."

"My feedings?" Kaitlyn asked. "It's okay, Logan. Come... see."

Kaitlyn ran out of the bathroom and headed down the hall. Logan jogged after her. She stopped before the door to her bedroom.

"Come on, Logan," she said, waving him in.

Logan entered the bedroom to find Kaitlyn dragging a cooler out from under her bed.

"Hey, where'd you get that cooler from?" he asked.

Kaitlyn pushed the cooler up before him and pulled back the lid. Inside, Logan discovered a wide array of meat products from meatballs to mini sausages.

"My food," Kaitlyn smiled.

"I can't believe it," Logan said. "You've been taking care of yourself the whole time! And I thought that maybe... you were..."

Logan paused and shook his head. Kaitlyn stared at him.

"I'm sorry," he said. "But when I first heard that Jeff Webber was missing, I thought that... that you ate him."

Kaitlyn's eyes grew large.

"Ate the boy?" she asked. "Oh, no, no, I don't do that."

Kaitlyn reached into the deep pocket on her sundress and pulled out a sneaker.

"The boy's," she said.

"Is that... is that Paul's sneaker?"

"No, it's the bad boy's," Kaitlyn grinned.

He looked at it. "Yup, that's Paul's sneaker all right. Well, we probably better give it back to him on Monday. I think a kindergarten-er scaring him is enough of a pay-back."

"Okay, Logan."

- 20 -

Numerous policemen populated the school hallway as Logan walked Kaitlyn to her classroom. Each officer wore a very concerned, stern face.

"This can't be good," Logan softly said.

"So many policemen," Kaitlyn marveled.

Upon reaching the entrance to Kaitlyn's classroom, the two found Mrs. Mahoney and Karen speaking to a police officer outside the doorway. Logan walked Kaitlyn right past the three adults, who barely acknowledged them.

Inside the classroom, all the kindergarteners were gathered on the large, square rug in the far left corner. Logan led Kaitlyn toward her desk.

"Okay, Kaitlyn, wait right here," he said, placing her book-bag down on the desk. "Mrs. Mahoney and Karen will be in here soon. I've gotta go now. Bye."

"Bye, Logan," Kaitlyn said, waving.

Logan exited the classroom. Kaitlyn looked over toward all the students that were crowding the far left corner. Everyone seemed to be frowning. Curious, Kaitlyn walked toward them.

"You're sad?" she asked the first girl to notice her.

"Miss Hammy's dead," the girl said between sorrowful sniffles.

Kaitlyn looked off toward the large cage on the windowsill that was Miss Hammy's home. The guinea pig was lying on her back with her eyes shut.

"Miss Hammy no longer lives?" Kaitlyn asked.

"Yes," the girl replied. "And it's very sad."

"No."

Kaitlyn marched off in the direction of the cage, pushing past student after mourning student. She hopped up on the windowsill and grabbed the cage's lid.

The students all emitted a collective gasp. Kaitlyn lifted off the lid and dropped it to the floor. She reached into the cage and picked Miss Hammy's floppy frame up.

"Don't do that!" yelled one student.

"Put her down!" exclaimed another. "That's sick!"

Ignoring the shouts, Kaitlyn lifted Miss Hammy up to her mouth. Some of the students screamed.

"Gross!" one cried. "She's going to eat it!"

With the entire mortified class looking on, Kaitlyn pressed her lips to Miss Hammy's furry back and took a gentle bite.

"She's doing it!" a student shouted. "She's eating Miss Hammy!"

Kaitlyn unclenched her jaw, revealing a tiny spot of blood at the side of her mouth, and slowly lowered Miss Hammy back into her cage. The guinea pig remained motionless amidst a pile of wood shavings. Suddenly, her legs twitched. The students screamed and Kaitlyn smiled.

"How?" a shocked student asked.

Everyone looked on as Miss Hammy stood up and took a little stroll around her cage.

"She's alive!" a student gasped. "Kaitlyn saved her!"

The classroom erupted in a booming barrage of cheers. Kaitlyn reached into her pocket and took out a small piece of ham. She dropped the piece of meat into Miss Hammy's food bowl.

The guinea pig noticed the food at once and rushed over to it. Kaitlyn hopped off the windowsill and was immediately met by a crowd of happy students congratulating her. The tiny spot of blood on the side of her mouth curved upwards as she emitted a huge smile.

"Class, please settle down," Mrs. Mahoney said, entering the room. "I have some very important news to tell you."

Down the hall, inside Logan's classroom, Mrs. Brissano stood before her students with a solemn face.

"Class, I was just informed the terrible news that there's been another kidnapping," she said. "Over the weekend, Paul Fallon was taken from Crabtree's Farm."

Logan's eyes widened.

Back in Kaitlyn's classroom, Mrs. Mahoney had just finished informing the students of Paul's kidnapping.

"Police officers will be circulating throughout the building all day today and there will be a brief assembly in one hour to further discuss what's going to be happening," Mrs. Mahoney said. "And, of course, if any of you know anything that can help with finding Paul, please let me or one of the policemen know."

Kaitlyn's eyes lit up with excitement. She reached inside her book bag and yanked out Paul's sneaker. She tapped Karen on the arm.

"What is it, Kaitlyn," Karen said, looking down at her.

"Paul!" Kaitlyn shouted, waving the sneaker in the air. "Paul!"

- 21-

Logan sat impatiently in the small lobby outside Principal Turner's office. He was joined by Logan's parents, Mrs. Mahoney, Karen, two policemen, and Kaitlyn behind the closed door. They had all gathered to go over Kaitlyn having Paul's sneaker.

Even though Logan had done his best trying to defend his sister when the sneaker was originally revealed that morning, it was not enough to convince the police officers or Principal Turner that Kaitlyn was innocent.

Everyone had been more concerned with the initial statements that were made to the students at the 10 a.m. assembly. Addressing the school behind the podium atop the stage in the large auditorium, Principal Turner stated that because of the second kidnapping, "There will be no more afterschool activities. Everyone is to proceed straight to the buses. If you don't take the bus, someone must be here to pick you up. There will be no outdoor recess as well. As for the upcoming Halloween festivities, the police have issued a 6 p.m. curfew so that all children will be at home before it gets dark. The mayor has also informed me that his son, Melvin the Magnificent, has cancelled his magic show scheduled for Halloween night."

Logan, as well of the rest of the students, weren't happy to hear all the new safety restrictions, though the general feeling throughout the school was that of fear.

Both Jeff and Paul, kids their age, were missing and no one seemed to know where to find them… and so far, Kaitlyn was the only lead.

The door to Principal Turner's office finally opened and the two policemen were the first to step out. Logan looked up from his seat just as his parents exited with Kaitlyn.

"Mom," he said and rushed up to her. "Can we go home now?"

"Yes, honey, we can," his mom replied and brushed her hand through his hair.

"Did they believe me? I told them Kaitlyn didn't do anything."

"Yes, Logan, we know," his dad answered. "Let's all just get home and get some rest."

- 22 -

"Happy birthday to you!" Mom sang as Kaitlyn came running down the stairs dressed in a pink princess costume.

"It's my birthday!" Kaitlyn shouted as she gave her mom a big hug.

"That's right, my little princess. Are you ready for some trick-or-treating?"

"Yeah! Yes! Candy!"

"But what about the parade?" Logan asked from the top of the stairs, dressed in a superhero costume.

"Some trick-or-treating first," Dad said, stepping up beside Mom and Kaitlyn. "Then the parade, then some more trick-or-treating!"

"And then cake at home for the birthday-girl," Mom added.

"My party!" Kaitlyn cheered. "Come on, Logan, let's go!"

Logan smiled and darted down the stairs. His red cape flapped wildly behind him. He snatched up a large, white pillowcase at the bottom of the steps.

"Okay!" he shouted. "Let's go!"

The entire family exited their home and out into the bright sunshine of Saturday afternoon. The sidewalks were already lined with young kids in costumes, each accompanied by one adult or more. Boisterous shouts of "trick or treat!" could be heard echoing forth from random front doorways and porches. Logan, Kaitlyn, and their parents happily joined in with the crowd. The vast ocean of trick-or-treaters flowed through the streets of

Hallowed Hills toward the town square where the parade would commence.

Dressed in a Dracula costume, Mayor Riggs greeted all the townspeople with a big smile and outstretched hands as they walked into the center of town.

"Welcome everyone," he said, shaking hands. "Thank you for coming. Enjoy yourselves. My son's got something special planned."

Staying close to Kaitlyn and his parents, Logan cast his eyes all about the town square, taking in all the fun and spooky sights. Halloween decorations were scattered about everywhere. Jack-o-lanterns lined the street. Buildings had ghosts painted on their windows. Life-sized skeletons took up residence on park benches. Standing next to a witch decoration, Lunch Lady Diana was passing out candy and drinks to all the little trick-or-treaters. Principal Turner was manning a pin-the-stem-on-the-pumpkin stand. Even Mrs. Brissano, Mrs. Mahoney and Karen were present, blowing up and handing out orange and black balloons.

Then Logan spotted Joe, dressed as a racecar driver, standing with his parents across the street. Kaitlyn tapped her brother on the arm

"There's Joe," she said, pointing.

Logan nodded as a girl from Kaitlyn's kindergarten class walked up to them.

"Hi, Kaitlyn!" she said.

"Hi, Beth," Kaitlyn waved back.

Logan's parents both looked down with shocked smiles, like it was the first time their daughter had ever been greeted by a child her own age—because it was.

"Do you want to come watch the parade with me?" Beth asked.

"Yes!" Kaitlyn smiled.

"We'll come with you and your parents," Logan's mom said.

"Okay, we're just over there," Beth replied, pointing at a spot on the sidewalk a mere ten feet away. "Kaitlyn brought Miss Hammy back to life."

"That's nice, dear," Mom said, not aware of exactly what Beth was talking about.

Logan's dad looked down at him.

"Come on, buddy," he said, patting Logan on the head. "Let's go watch the parade with Kaitlyn's friend."

"But, Dad, Joe is just over there across the street," Logan whined. "Can't I go watch the parade with him?"

"We'll stop over by Joe when the parade's over and go trick-or-treating with him and his parents. Sound good?"

"Okay, Dad."

"Good boy. Come on, let's go. I think the parade's about to start.

Logan's dad took Kaitlyn's hand.

"Okay, honey," Dad said. "Let's walk over to your friend."

"We're not going to Joe?" Kaitlyn asked.

"Not now. We're going to hang out with your friend, Beth."

"Okay! Yay!"

Kaitlyn skipped over toward Beth, dragging her father along. Logan quietly followed as Mayor Riggs stepped up to his announcer's podium off in the distance.

"Happy Halloween, my fellow Hallowed Hill-toppers!" the mayor spoke into a microphone. "I hope everyone's in a fun, festive mood!"

The crowd clapped and cheered as the last of the arrivals quickly filed into the square.

"Our great town shares a great history with this holiday," Mayor Riggs went on. "For many years, our forefathers have carried forth the fine institution of celebrating All Hallows Eve. Today, it warms my heart to see us all continuing in that great tradition. So... let the parade begin!"

Some creepily playful organ music began blasting forth from a huge set of speakers. All the children in the crowd squealed with excitement.

"Look!" Logan exclaimed, pointing down the street.

A float with a gigantic tarantula on top was driving their way. The arachnid's eight long legs moved up and down with the help of some puppetry strings attached to them. The crowd roared with approval as the float passed them by, followed by a marching band dressed as skeletons and playing *Monster Mash.*

The procession of floats and patrons went on for quite some time, showcasing one amazing Halloween-themed display after the next. Buckets of candy were thrown out to all the cheerful, costumed children. As the tail end of the parade drew near, Logan spotted someone wearing a large top hat standing atop the final float.

"Here comes Melvin the Magnificent," he said.

"Magic man?" Kaitlyn shouted.

Two large rows of long sparklers ignited along the sides of the magician's float. Melvin extracted a magic wand from up his sleeve and began waving it like the conductor of a symphony.

A hazy mist sprayed forth from the wand. The audience expressed great awe. Melvin spun his wand around and around, causing the mist to transform its shape.

"It's a ghost!" shouted out a child.

The crowd gasped as a smoky specter was indeed rising up out of the wand's tip. The trick aroused a healthy row of applause.

Melvin spun the wand in a few small, circular motions and released the ghost up into the air. The wand then shot back up his sleeve. Melvin clapped his hands together and began rolling them over each other. His palms moved faster and faster until a spark lit up between them, revealing a deck of playing cards.

"Let's play a card game!" he grinned.

The audience applauded their approval. Melvin shuffled the cards back and forth. His fingertips gracefully spun the deck up and down, left and right.

The more he shuffled, the farther apart his hands grew. Once his palms were about a shoulder's length away, Melvin sprayed the cards into the pattern of a pumpkin.

"Wow!" Logan grinned.

While still spewing the cards back and forth, Melvin shifted his hands slightly, causing the pumpkin to form the face of a jack-o-lantern. A tiny spark burst out of the center of the circular array of cards.

The jack-o-lantern now appeared to have a glowing candle inside its mouth. Melvin shuffled the cards a bit longer to allow the entire audience to get a good look at his trick.

Once satisfied, he forcefully clapped his hands. The candle and the jack-o-lantern were immediately compressed back into a small deck of cards. The audience erupted into a huge ovation.

"That's my boy!" Mayor Riggs proudly blared into the microphone.

Melvin bent the deck a bit and aimed it out at the audience. With a tiny slip of his fingertips, the cards went squirting into the air like the bullets of a machine gun.

The crowd shouted with glee as fifty-two rectangular cards rained down upon them. Everyone attempted to catch them as souvenirs.

Logan watched from a ways off as Joe grabbed one of the magical souvenirs for himself.

"Aw, lucky!" Logan said. "I wish he threw those cards over here by me."

Kaitlyn looked in the same direction as her brother to see Joe waving the card around and smiling.

"Joe got it," she said.

- 23 -

Volunteer workers began cleaning up the aftermath of the parade once Melvin's float had exited the town square. Little, wrapped-up pieces of candy and confetti were sprinkled sporadically around the street and sidewalks.

A great deal of the crowd had already filed out of the area and the sun was showing signs of setting. Logan and his family were on their way toward Joe and his parents.

"Okay, everyone," Logan's dad said. "We'll meet up with Joe's family, do a few more blocks of trick-or-treating, then go home."

"That's right," Mom nodded. "I want us back in the house before it gets dark."

"Then let's hurry!" Logan shouted and began running. "We have to get more candy!"

"Yeah, candy!" Kaitlyn happily repeated and darted after her brother.

Logan was the first to reach Joe and his parents.

"Hey," Joe smiled. "Did you see Melvin the Magnificent?"

"He was great!" Logan said. "I can't believe you got one of his cards!"

"I know." Joe held up the playing card.

"Maybe he'll autograph it for you," Joe's dad suggested.

Logan and Joe's eyes lit up.

"You think so?" Logan asked.

"Sure, we'll stop by the magic shop tomorrow," Joe's dad replied. "But now, I think we should all finish up our trick-or-treating."

"Great idea," Logan's dad smiled. "We were just thinking the same thing."

"Candy!" Kaitlyn shouted.

"That's right, honey," Mom said, patting her daughter's head. "Let's head out everyone."

The group began to walk toward the town square's exit. Joe went to put the playing card in his pocket but a quick gust of wind abruptly swept the card out of his hand.

"Hey!" Joe yelled. "My card!"

Joe and Logan watched as the playing card floated along the sidewalk. No one else took notice.

"Go get it," Logan insisted.

"Be right back," Joe said and sprinted down the sidewalk.

"Where's Joe going?" Kaitlyn asked.

"Just to get his card," Logan answered.

Kaitlyn kept her gaze on Joe as her father walked up to them.

"Look at what I found, Logan," Dad said, holding up another one of Melvin's magical playing cards.

"Yes!" Logan shouted. "Thanks, Dad!"

Logan charged forward and grabbed hold of the card. Everyone laughed except for Kaitlyn who was still focusing on Joe. The escaping card sailed quickly along through the air.

"Get back here!" Joe called, reaching out his hands.

The card took an awkward turn to the right just as Joe was about to snatch it. Kaitlyn chuckled at the near miss and took a few steps toward him.

The card zipped down an alleyway between a bookstore and Melvin's magic shop. Joe disappeared around the bend.

The alleyway was closed off from most of the day's fading sunlight. All that occupied the small section was a green dumpster, a few dented trash cans, and a couple of cardboard boxes and crates.

Still, Joe had no trouble finding his card, which was strangely stuck to the front of the dumpster. The small white card stuck out easily on the green metal background. Joe reached out for it.

That was when the lid of the dumpster suddenly sprung open. Before Joe could even look up, he was lifted off the ground.

Kaitlyn rounded the bend in the alley just in time to see Joe's feet disappear into the dumpster and the lid slam shut. Confused, she took one step into the alley and stopped.

"Joe?" she softly called.

There was no reply.

Kaitlyn went scurrying down the alley and noticed right away that the playing card was still stuck to the dumpster.

"Joe?" she repeated. "Are you in there? Did you fall in?"

After a second response of silence, Kaitlyn climbed up on a large crate and was soon staring down at the dumpster's lid. She gently lifted it up.

The inside of the dumpster was very dark. She stared and saw a small, slightly open trap door and a ladder leading downward.

"Fun!" she smiled.

Thinking that Joe was playing some sort of game, she hopped inside the darkened dumpster and opened up the trap door. A ladder leading downward was revealed. She carefully stepped onto the first rung and began climbing down.

Her shoes only traveled a few feet before striking the ground. She turned away from the ladder to find a long, dimly lit tunnel.

"Joe?" Kaitlyn called, her voice echoing through the tunnel. When she didn't hear a reply from Joe, she raced forward.

"He's far ahead!" she playfully yelled. "He's winning! I have to catch up!"

The tunnel winded around a small bend and ended at the base of another ladder.

"I'm going to find you, Joe!" she said, dancing up to the new ladder.

She climbed up the not-too-tall ladder and found another trap door at the top. Kaitlyn pressed her hands into the door and felt it easily give way. She peeked her head up and out to find a darkened, rundown room. Wooden beams and dusty drop cloths were scattered across the floor.

"Joe?" Kaitlyn whispered. "Where are you?"

There was no answer. The entire room was quiet until a loud gurgling sang out from Kaitlyn's belly.

Oh, I'm hungry, she thought.

Suddenly a loud thud occurred a little ways off in the darkness. Kaitlyn quickly covered her mouth, a tad startled.

"Is that you, Joe?" she asked, cautiously stepping out onto the floor.

An odd clinking sound was returned. By now, Kaitlyn's eyes had adjusted to the darkness and could tell that nothing else was moving before her in the room. Feeling less nervous, she jogged toward the other side of the room and soon reached a large curtain.

She could now hear many more sounds. There was grunting, sniffling, more clinking, and thumping... and all directly behind the curtain. Captivated, she crept up to the curtain and delicately pulled back a small portion.

"Keep quiet!" she heard a deafening voice yell from bellow.

Kaitlyn halted her hold on the curtain and crouched down on her knees. She carefully snuck one eye around the clouded fabric, and thanks to the much brighter second room, immediately spotted Joe. He was trapped inside a steel cage hanging in the air. Someone was hoisting him up high using a rope pulley system.

Kaitlyn normally would have laughed at such an odd sight, but Joe appeared to have tears in his eyes. She also noticed two other boys strung up in cages similar to Joe's—Jeff and Paul, the two boys that Kaitlyn remembered were missing.

They both had frightened expressions on their faces and made little whimpering sounds.

"I said keep quiet!" bellowed the man as he finished lifting Joe's cage. He tied the rope to a large bolt sticking up from the floor.

He had his back turned to Kaitlyn, so she couldn't see his face. He was also wearing a long, black cloak with a large hood that further kept her from distinguishing who he was. Curious, she stepped out from behind the curtain to find herself standing on a stage platform.

"Who are you?" she innocently asked the cloaked figure.

Startled, the man spun around, causing the black hood to fling off, revealing a tall top hat. Kaitlyn hopped back slightly upon seeing Melvin the Magnificent glaring at her with wide, insane eyes.

"You," he exhaled. "Where did you come from, Kaitlyn?"

"Is this part of the game?" she asked.

"Game?" The magician was perplexed.

"The hide and seek game I was playing with Joe."

"No, Kaitlyn!" Joe shouted. "This isn't a game! You have to..."

"Be quiet!" Melvin yelled and slapped the base of Joe's cage with a jangling set of metal keys.

He got down on one knee before Kaitlyn.

"Yes, dear, this is a game and we're about to win," he smiled.

Kaitlyn quietly gazed at Melvin's bloodshot eyes.

"We win?" she asked, turning her sights to the three boys in the cages.

"That's right," Melvin said. "I'm not sure how you arrived, but it's only fair that you're here for it. Did anyone else come with you?"

"No, just me."

"Good."

The magician took hold of Kaitlyn's hand, causing her eyes to look away from the boys.

"Don't listen to him, Kaitlyn!" Joe shouted. "He's a bad man! Run and get help!"

Melvin instantly spun around and hurled his keys at Joe's cage. The metal bars let out a loud clank as the keys connected, forcing Joe to silence.

"Not another word," Melvin growled.

He looked away from Joe to see Kaitlyn scurrying back toward the curtain.

"Hey, Kaitlyn, don't run off," he called out and took three long, swift strides after her.

He easily caught up to her and retook hold of her hand.

"I can't go?" she asked.

"There's no need for that, dear," Melvin answered.

He led Kaitlyn over to a folding chair near the edge of the stage. Melvin picked her up and plopped her down on the cushioned seat.

He pulled some twine out of his pocket and began wrapping it around Kaitlyn and the chair.

"Why are you tying me up?" she asked.

"I just want to make sure you don't fall off the chair," he grinned.

His hands returned to the twine and finished tying her up.

"There we are," he said. "Safe and sound. Now we can let the birthday celebration begin!"

"Hey, today's *my* birthday!" Kaitlyn smiled.

"I know," the magician nodded and stepped away from her.

Melvin walked over to the three caged boys and picked up the keys. He adjusted his top hat and spun back around to face Kaitlyn.

"And you know what else?" he asked her. "It's my birthday, too!"

Kaitlyn's eyes widened. "Really?" she asked. "Today is your birthday? Wow! Two people with the same birthday!"

"Yes, that's right!" Melvin grinned, partially tipping his top hat. "But... it's someone else's birthday, too."

"Another?"

"Uh-huh, another."

He slapped Joe's cage, causing it to jostle back and forth from its hanging position.

"Stop it!" Joe yelled. "Kaitlyn, get out of those ropes and go get help! He locked us all up here with those keys!"

"Quiet!" Melvin hollered and violently grabbed onto Joe's cage.

He brought the cage close to his face and glared maniacally at Joe.

"So, now you want *her* help?" Melvin began, "Why, just a short while ago, weren't you mad at her for ruining your birthday?" He glanced over at Paul and Jeff. "And you two were also quick to point out that Kaitlyn was different and thus, perfect for being made fun of."

Melvin released his grip on the cage and walked back toward Kaitlyn.

"Everyone in this town seems to have some sort of prejudice toward this little girl," he continued. "Just because she's a little different." He looked back at the boys. "Does this sound fair to you? Well, does it?"

All three boys began to sniffle as their eyes welled up with tears. Melvin let out a loud laugh.

"Ha!" he snorted. "Yes, that's what you do. You cry because you know you're wrong. I expect everyone else in town to do the same thing once they realize the error of their ways. I heard the same kind of taunts when I was a boy and no one did anything for me then. My father could only take me out of school... keep me hidden... make everyone forget about me. Now, I'll make them remember..."

Melvin inhaled a deep sniff through his nose as if he'd called to mind some painful past event. He shook his head hard to break free from the rude recollection, causing his top hat to nearly fall off. His hand rapidly shot up and balanced the brim before it toppled off his head.

"Enough talk of the past," Melvin said. "Let's start the birthday festivities!"

"Yay!" Kaitlyn shouted. "Our birthdays! Where's the other one?"

"Funny, you should ask, my dear." Melvin walked closer to her. "I was just about to reveal him to you and everyone else."

"Oh, goodie!"

"Yes, you should be excited. He's someone very much like you, Kaitlyn. I'm so glad you finally get to meet him."

"Where is he?" Kaitlyn's eyes were wide with anticipation.

"He's very close. I'm going to magically make him appear." Melvin extended his hands toward both Kaitlyn and the caged boys. "Lady and gentlemen, here's Lewis... my brother!"

The four children looked all about the stage area. No one else was there.

"Where is he?" Kaitlyn asked.

"My brother?" Melvin asked. "My *twin* brother?"

He brought both hands to the brim of his top hat. A sinister smile formed across his lips before they parted to say, "Why, he's... right... here!"

Melvin lifted the top hat off his head. The boys immediately let out shrieks of fright and slid to the backs of their cages. Attached to the top of Melvin's head was another smaller head and a long, skinny arm! Its skin was darker than the magician's and had a greenish tint. Its nearly bald head sprouted a few messy strands of hair.

"Yes, that was the typical reaction people gave when I was young," Melvin mournfully recalled. "And the main reason my father switched me to home schooling."

The continuous screams of the boys prevented them from hearing Melvin's speech in its entirety. Lewis stretched out his single, scraggly arm and emitted a deep yawn. His movements ceased the boys' hysterics as silence overcame each of them.

"You're not tired, are you, brother?" Melvin asked, looking upwards. "I've set up a wonderful birthday celebration for you."

"It's so dark inside that hat," Lewis said, his voice droning at a very low octave.

"Yes, I know, but I promise it'll be worth the wait. Your present is ready for you."

"That's wonderful," Lewis smiled with his jagged teeth and then looked over at Kaitlyn. "Is she the one you told me about?"

He pointed a single skinny digit at her. Melvin turned so that they were both fully facing Kaitlyn. Her eyes were wide in childish wonderment.

"Oh, you mean our little surprise guest?" Melvin said. "Yes, that's her! And we're so lucky she showed up, don't you think? Kaitlyn, don't you have anything to say?"

Kaitlyn kept her amazed vision focused squarely on the hatless magician.

"You have a little green guy on top of your head," she said naively.

"Yes, I do," Melvin chuckled. "He's my twin brother. My Siamese twin brother."

"What's size-ma-see?" Kaitlyn asked.

"It means we were both born at the same time, only connected."

Kaitlyn turned her head to the side, slowly processing Melvin's words.

"Then why are you still connected?" she asked.

"My, you sure are inquisitive," Melvin smiled. "I wonder if the other people in town know that about you. Kaitlyn, we're still connected because Lewis and I share part of the same brain. If a doctor tried to separate us, we would both die."

"Oh, no!"

"That's right, it would be terrible. Therefore, Lewis and I have to stay together... forever."

"Forever," Lewis hissed.

"Thank you for understanding the seriousness of our situation, dear," Melvin said. "It's too bad that the people in town didn't, but I'm sure you know what I'm talking about."

"Me?" Kaitlyn asked. "I know?"

"You're a lot like Lewis and me," Melvin said, kneeling down before her. "Well, more like Lewis, as he's the one that got the meat craving, not me. I believe that anyone born in this town on Halloween has a great deal in common. I understand that you have quite the taste for meat, am I right, Kaitlyn?"

"I like meatballs and hot dogs and burgers."

"Yes, of course, but I bet you like *another* kind of meat even more!"

"What do you mean?"

"Our kind was meant to enjoy human flesh!" Lewis interrupted. "It's what we were born to do in order to survive."

"Yes, Lewis, yes," Melvin said. "That's how it's meant to be, but you see, Kaitlyn, we were all born into this town with this need... yet it's considered wrong by everyone else in town *not* born on Halloween."

"As if it was *our* fault!" Lewis hollered.

"Eating people?" Kaitlyn gasped. "But it's wrong to eat people. My brother told me." Melvin then swooped down before her so Kaitlyn was nearly eye-to-eye with Lewis.

"Your brother is just a boy," Melvin growled. "He's the one who's wrong. Because of people like him, I've had to resort to putrid meat substitutes to feed my brother, like meatballs, hot dogs, and other processed junk."

"I like hot dogs," Kaitlyn smiled.

"Hot dogs aren't what we need," Lewis said. "Look at me!"

Lewis pointed at his ugly green skin and few hair strands.

"The best source of nutrients for you and Lewis," Melvin said, "is the freshest, strongest meat there is... young children."

Kaitlyn's jaw dropped and she fiercely shook her head from side to side. The three boys trembled feverishly in their cages.

"Oh, no!" she yelled. "That's bad!"

"No, it's not, Kaitlyn!" Lewis shouted back. "It's a better life for you and me. It's survival of the fittest. We are what we are."

"Yes, you are," Melvin nodded, pulling out the set of keys. "And believe me, I know how hard it can be to resist; to know that once you bite another living thing that it causes that living thing to change... to be more like you. *Zombie* is what many would call it, but I say it's just natural selection. Regardless, I think it's time to celebrate your birthday properly, brother."

The magician turned toward the hanging cages, allowing Lewis to gain a full, frontal view. The boys once again retreated deeper into the back end of their cages.

"Now, Lewis," Melvin said, aiming one key at the cages, "which of your three birthday presents would you like to eat first?"

Lewis's beady eyes surveyed Paul, Jeff, and Joe. A grin grew across his green face. "That one," he said, aiming his frail index finger at Joe.

"No!" Joe shouted. "Help!"

"Shut your mouth!" Melvin hollered. "My brother needs proper nourishment and you get to be the first one to give it to him. You're helping him. Try thinking of it that way."

He began walking closer to Joe, extending the key. He sang a cheery tune with each step.

"Happy birthday to you." He patted the back of Lewis's head. "Happy birthday to you. Happy birthday, dear Lewis. Happy birth..."

"Hungry!" Kaitlyn cried out.

Melvin stopped walking and slowly looked over his shoulder.

"I'm hungry," Kaitlyn repeated. "I want meat... the good kind."

Lewis reached his single, scrawny arm down and tapped his brother's shoulder.

"Melvin, is she asking me to share my birthday gift with her?" he asked.

"Um, yes, brother," Melvin replied. "She is."

Lewis smiled.

"Well then, untie her!" he said. "This is a celebration for all those of our kind."

Without saying another word, Melvin placed the set of keys inside his cloak and kneeled down before Kaitlyn. He began loosening the twine wrapped around her.

"Come," he said, "enjoy your meal with Lewis."

Melvin lifted her up in his arms. Kaitlyn was now directly below Lewis' chin. She could actually see his lips salivating with anticipation of feeding.

"Get ready for something amazing," Lewis grinned.

"I'm ready to eat," Kaitlyn bravely assured him as she tightly gripped Melvin's cloak.

As the magician approached Joe's cage, Kaitlyn took notice of the rope that was holding it up. The rope ran up to a second level balcony above the stage before heading back down to the bolt in the floor it was tied to.

"It's time to dine," Melvin said, stopping right before Joe's cage.

He switched Kaitlyn into his other arm and reached his free hand inside his cloak.

"Hurry, brother," Lewis said. "I'm starving."

"I know, Lewis," Melvin replied. "I'm just looking for... the key. I put it right here in my inside pocket. Where are my keys?"

A small, bright light quickly flashed across the magician's face. Melvin looked up to see Kaitlyn dangling the shiny set of keys.

"Oh, you have them," he said to her. "Okay, give them here. I'm unlocking your supper."

Kaitlyn gave him a little smirk and angrily furrowed her eyebrows.

"My brother is right!" she shouted. "You are wrong!"

Kaitlyn swung the set of keys upward into Lewis' jaw. The green-skinned monster screamed in pain, causing Melvin to awkwardly drop his young hostage to the floor.

Kaitlyn landed on both feet, keys still in hand, and sprinted over to the rope's anchoring bolt. She grabbed the thick twine with her free hand, opened her mouth of hearty chompers, and bit down.

Her sharp bite immediately severed the rope, causing Joe's cage to fall to the floor. Melvin and Lewis rushed toward Kaitlyn, but the rapidly moving rope whisked her up in the air. She tightly held on as her feet soared over the magician and his brother.

"Get her!" Melvin yelled and jumped into the air.

Lewis stretched out his single, skinny arm, but merely grazed the bottom of Kaitlyn's left foot as she went sailing up to the second level balcony above the stage.

"I missed her!" Lewis hollered. "She has the keys! I'm starving!"

"Don't worry, Lewis," Melvin assured him. "She won't get far. There's no place to go on the second floor."

- 24 -

Kaitlyn's feet touched down on the second floor platform above the stage, the cage's keys jingling in her hand. She released her grip on the rope, sending it careening back down to the first floor.

"Run, Kaitlyn!" Joe called up to her.

Kaitlyn heard footsteps rapidly ascending her way. She hurried off the platform and entered a darkened room with a desk, chairs, and boxes scattered across the floor.

The room had one window, and the sky outside had turned dark, leaving little light for Kaitlyn to proceed properly.

Fortunately, she did see a light switch on the wall beside her and flipped it on. The room remained dark, but a large beam of brightness erupted outside, resembling the beam of a spotlight.

"She's in the office!" Melvin's voice echoed. He sounded like he was getting closer.

She rushed to the window and looked outside. The spotlight on the ground had been turned on.

Everyone will know where I am when the lights are on, Kaitlyn thought. *People will come.*

She opened the window and took a long look downwards. The ground appeared very far off.

I'm up so high, she thought.

Suddenly, Melvin and Lewis barged into the room.

"She's over there by the window!" Lewis yelled, extending a bony finger.

Melvin ran toward her. Kaitlyn tried to move out of the way, but was roughly tackled by the charging magician.

They hit the floor hard. Kaitlyn landed on her back and looked up at the two troublesome twin brothers.

"Give me those keys!" Melvin demanded.

She raised the ring of jingling keys high in the air. Melvin's eyes lit up as he reached for the shiny set. Before he could grab them, Kaitlyn tossed them out the window.

"No!" Melvin screamed.

"Get them!" Lewis hollered.

Melvin jumped off Kaitlyn and extended his hand. He reached out the window and swiped at the falling keys.

He missed, lost his balance, and began falling forward.

"Melvin, look out!" Lewis warned.

He tried to reach back at the windowsill, but it was too late.

"Lewis!" Melvin yelled.

Lewis attempted to hold onto the edge of the window, but his frail fingers couldn't get a good grip.

Melvin screamed in shocked alarm as he tumbled into the air.

The spotlight intermittently lit up his falling body as it fell. A spray of playing cards went floating out from his pockets, flying off in all directions.

He was screaming the entire time.

Then the screaming ceased and there was a muffled *thud*.

Kaitlyn jumped to her feet and ran to the window. Below, Melvin's lifeless body was sprawled across the top of his theater's marquee; playing cards gently landed around him.

Kaitlyn hurried down the second floor stairwell until she was back on the lower level stage.

Joe, Jeff, and Paul remained anxiously in their cages as a crowd of adults rushed into the theater, including Logan and his parents.

"It's the missing boys!" shouted a member of the crowd.

Kaitlyn slowly stepped out onto the stage.

"It's that strange little girl!" called out another member of the crowd. "She did something to the boys!"

"No!" Joe barked at the top of his lungs. "Kaitlyn didn't do anything wrong! Melvin the Magnificent kidnapped us. Kaitlyn saved us all!"

Kaitlyn smiled out at the audience and she was immediately greeted by Logan. He jumped onto the stage and lifted her up in a huge hug.

Back outside, atop the marquee, the people rushing into the magic shop did not see Melvin's motionless body overhead. The commotion on the ground caused Lewis' eyes to shoot open. He glanced down at his brother's still body.

"Melvin?" he said.

The magician's lips didn't move.

"Melvin!" Lewis persisted. "Answer me!"

Melvin remained silent. Lewis mournfully glanced down at his brother's wrist, which was lying directly next to him.

"Melvin," he began, "I won't let you die."

Lewis grabbed his brother's arm and opened his mouth. With feverish determination, he brought the bare arm to his shiny, sharp teeth.

- 26 -

Mayor Riggs stood solemnly before a podium in front of his large mansion. A large group of Hallowed Hills patrons gathered on the lawn before him. With a brief nod, the mayor leaned in toward the microphone atop the podium.

"My fellow Hallowed Hill-toppers," he exhaled. "In regards to what took place this past Halloween evening at Melvin's magic shop, I'd like to extend my sincerest apologies to the families of the children that were involved. Though I was completely unaware of the terrible actions my son committed, I still can't help but feel somewhat responsible."

The mayor looked away from the microphone and brought a white handkerchief up to his tearing eyes.

"I care so very much for all the people of this great town," he continued after wiping away the tears. "I'd never wish harm on any of them and just... knowing that what happened was caused by someone so close to me..." he trailed off and brought the handkerchief back up to his sorrowful face.

"It just makes me feel terrible," he said. "I hope you can find it in your hearts to forgive me. And although the police haven't been able to located Melvin's whereabouts, I won't rest until he's found... and brought to justice."

The crowd immediately gave off a rousing row of applause. The mayor pounded his fist into the podium.

"Even though Melvin's my son, I understand that his actions must be accounted for. He must learn that is *not* the way an upstanding citizen conducts himself in Hallowed Hills! He will be punished!"

The patrons once again clapped their strong approval.

"Thank you, everyone," the mayor smiled. "Thank you so very much. With your support, I still plan to continue serving as your mayor to the best of my ability. I hope to see you all at the celebratory ceremony being held in the center of town in honor of our heroic, young resident, Kaitlyn."

The mayor stepped down from the podium amidst a burst of cheers. He waved out at the crowd and gave them a thumbs-up before walking back to the front door of his mansion.

"Thank you, one and all," he waved before entering his home.

As the front door closed, the audience began leaving the lawn. Mayor Riggs watched secretly behind the curtains of one of the mansion's first floor windows as everyone left, some stopping and chatting amongst themselves for a while.

Two hours later, when the last patron was finally gone, he walked to a door underneath a grand stairway. His hand carefully turned the knob and pulled the door open, revealing a long staircase.

The darkened steps let out little creeks as he descended. Upon reaching the basement, he turned on a light with the switch mounted to the wall. A bulb in the ceiling began to flicker, illuminating a small white refrigerator.

He kneeled down before the refrigerator and opened it, then extracted a large plastic bag. He kicked the refrigerator door closed with the back of his foot.

A loud moan suddenly came echoing through the basement. The mayor sighed glumly and trudged toward a thick-looking metal doorway at the other end of the room. There was no doorknob, just a strange circular keyhole in the center. A second moan gurgled forth from behind the door. He took a key from his pocket and inserted it into the hole. The door made a little click sound and then popped open.

The freshly breached gap instantly allowed another, much louder moan to escape. The mayor rolled his eyes and entered the doorway. He opened the plastic bag and held it with two hands. The moaning ceased.

"I think they all believed me," the mayor said, taking two steps forward.

After turning on a light hanging from the ceiling, he reached inside the plastic bag and took out a large container of raw hamburger meat. Another moan was emitted that quickly turned into a salivating slurp.

"I know you're hungry," the mayor said. "It wasn't easy being seen in public buying meat. I had to be very careful."

After unwrapping the meat, he tossed it into a darkened corner of the room. The sound of ravenous chomping rapidly occurred.

"Yes, eat up," the mayor said. "I know how this works. I just wish you'd let me know about your plan involving the children. We could have devised a much safer solution. Now look what's happened to you." He looked toward the cement floor and shook his head. "I don't know how we're going to move forward, but I'll think of something."

The chomping sound stopped. The mayor took another container of raw meat out of the bag and threw it at the corner of the room. A greenish-pale hand shot forth from the darkness and caught the meat.

Melvin's face forcefully emerged from the shadows and took a huge bite out of the still-unopened package. Lewis sat atop his head, reaching out his lone, skinny arm.

"Make sure your brother gets some, too," the mayor scolded Melvin. "If it wasn't for him, you wouldn't even be here."

Melvin balled-up a piece of meat and flung it upwards. Lewis caught the ball in his mouth, nearly swallowing it whole.

"Thank you, brother," Lewis said. "And, Father, don't be mad at Melvin. He's still getting used to the transformation."

"Yes, Lewis, I understand," the mayor said. "I just wish he'd been more cautious. It wasn't easy keeping you hidden all these years, but we got through it by working together. Melvin strayed from that path and now we're in a very worrisome situation."

"I'm sorry, Father," Melvin said as bits of meat flew from his mouth. "I didn't mean to hurt the family. I wanted to send a message to those that disrespect the nature of the ones born on Halloween."

"I know that, Melvin," the mayor nodded. "You can't let your emotions get the best of you. Yes, it's not easy, but look what happened? You were defeated by your own kind... and she was only a child!"

Melvin lowered his head in shame, forcing Lewis to do the same. The mayor exhaled a deep groan of frustration.

"How long do we have to stay locked down here?" Melvin asked.

"I don't know," Mayor Riggs replied. "At least until you're able to somehow control your appetite. I can't have you running around like a mad man searching for meat all over town. It'll ruin everything we've worked for. I need some time to think things through. For now, you two have to stay here, out of the public eye. Got it?"

Melvin and Lewis both looked back.

"Yes, Father," Melvin frowned.

"Yes, Father," Lewis repeated.

"Good boys," the mayor nodded. "I'll be back in a little while with more food. Till then, try and keep calm. I now have to go and give an award to that awful little girl, Kaitlyn."

Melvin remained silent as his father stepped out of the room and closed the door behind him. The sound of the lock clicking in place came soon after. Once the mayor's footsteps faded off in the distance, Lewis glanced down at his brother.

"Don't worry, Melvin," Lewis said. "You'll get used to your new state of mind and body. Soon you'll be able to manage the hunger pains. You'll also realize a newfound strength as well as other greater abilities. Just wait, you'll see... and when you're ready, we'll take care of that terrible little girl, Kaitlyn. And we'll to it together!"

- 27 -

Kaitlyn and Logan were in the back seat of their car as they headed with their parents toward the center of town. They were dressed in their *fancy occasion* clothes.

"Are you excited, Kaitlyn?" Dad asked from the driver's seat.

"I don't know," Kaitlyn smiled innocently.

"Well, we certainly are," Mom said from the passenger's side. "It's going to be a wonderful ceremony in your honor."

"Ceremony?" Kaitlyn asked.

"She just means a party," Logan informed her. "A great big party for my sister, the superhero!"

Kaitlyn grinned big and quietly rested the side of her head on her brother's shoulder.

"We're all so proud of you, honey," Dad said.

"So's the whole town!" Logan exclaimed. "Everyone's talking about how brave she is! Now everyone wants to be her friend. It's so much better than it was before."

"What do you mean by before?" Mom asked.

Logan glanced down at his sister, still leaning on his shoulder.

"I just mean that it took some people a while to understand just how special Kaitlyn is," Logan explained. "Just because she's a little different doesn't mean she's still not a normal kid."

"I think you two make a great team," Dad said. "And I'm glad that everything will finally be getting back to normal around here."

He happily honked the horn on the steering wheel, causing Logan and Kaitlyn to laugh. With the sky darkening, the car sped off in the direction of the town center, passing by Crabtree's Farm.

The honked horn startled a few of the cows, causing them to let out some loud mooing. Farmer Crabtree came rushing out from the nearby barn, holding a bright lantern.

"What's the matter, girls?" he said to the cows. "Something got you spooked?"

The farmer looked out across the pasture. All appeared to be quiet.

"It's okay, girls," he said. "Nothing out here but the grass you love to eat."

The cows lowered their heads back to the ground and began chewing up small clumps of grass. Farmer Crabtree lowered his lantern, unaware of the gentle hooves creeping up behind him.

"There's nothing to be afraid of," he said.

The cow behind the farmer suddenly exhaled a rough snort from its pink spotted nose, spraying a light mist over the back of his head. Startled, Farmer Crabtree froze in his boots.

"My cows don't ever do that," he nervously uttered, lifting up the lantern.

The cow, displaying the scar of Kaitlyn's bite mark across its skin, leaned in closer to the back of the farmer's fleshy neck.

Its eyes were glowing green.

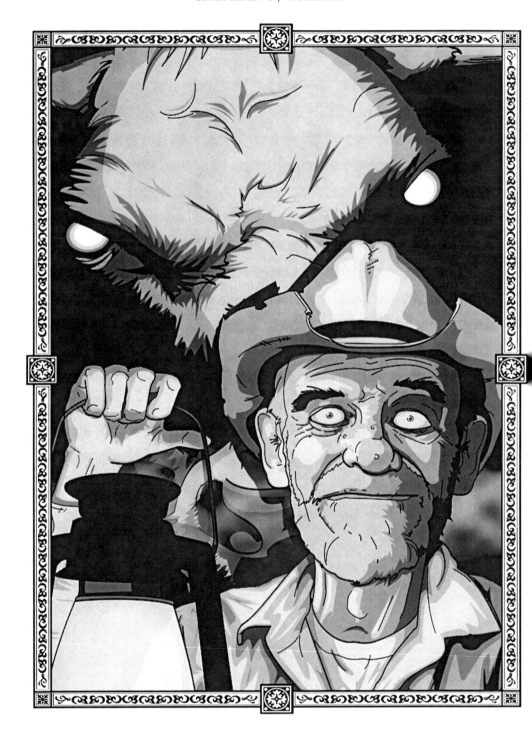

THE WAR AGAINST THEM: A ZOMBIE NOVEL
by Jose Alfredo Vazquez

Mankind wasn't prepared for the onslaught.

An ancient organism is reanimating the dead bodies of its victims, creating worldwide chaos and panic as the disease spreads to every corner of the globe. As governments struggle to contain the disease, courageous individuals across the planet learn what it truly means to make choices as they struggle to survive.

Geopolitics meet technology in a race to save mankind from the worst threat it has ever faced. Doctors, military and soldiers from all walks of life battle to find a cure. For the dead walk, and if not stopped, they will wipe out all life on Earth. Humanity is fighting a war they cannot win, for who can overcome Death itself? Man versus the walking dead with the winner ruling the planet. Welcome to *The War Against Them*.

THE TURNING: A STORY OF THE LIVING DEAD
by Kelly M. Hudson

The Dead Walk!

And no place on earth is safe from their ravening hunger. Civilization falls, leaving groups of struggling survivors to navigate a world that has descended into Hell.

Jeff Richards is one such survivor. He and his lover Jenny flee their home in the Bay Area and take a perilous journey through Northern California into Oregon, seeking shelter in rural areas to avoid both the living dead and that most treacherous animal of all: their fellow humans.

But can a man who has lost everything, including his humanity, ever be reborn? When the dead walk, will any of us survive?

Or will we all join the ranks of the undead to forever walk the earth.

END OF DAYS: AN APOCALYPTIC ANTHOLOGY VOLUMES 1-3

Edited by Anthony Giangregorio

Our world is a fragile place.

Meteors, famine, floods, nuclear war, solar flares, and hundreds of other calamities can plunge our small blue planet into turmoil in an instant.

What would you do if tomorrow the sun went super nova or the world was swallowed by water, submerging the world into the cold darkness of the ocean? This anthology explores some of those scenarios and plunges you into total annihilation. But remember, it's only a book, and tomorrow will come as it always does.

Or will it?

KINGDOM OF THE DEAD
by Anthony Giangregorio
THE DEAD HAVE RISEN!

In the dead city of Pittsburgh, two small enclaves struggle to survive, eking out an existence of hand to mouth.

But instead of working together, both groups battle for the last remaining fuel and supplies of a city filled with the living dead.

Six months after the initial outbreak, a lone helicopter arrives bearing two more survivors and a newborn baby. One enclave welcomes them, while the other schemes to steal their helicopter and escape the decaying city.

With no police, fire, or social services existing, the two will battle for dominance in the steel city of the walking dead. But when the dust settles, the question is: will the remaining humans be the winners, or the losers?

When the dead walk, the line between Heaven and Hell is so twisted and bent there is no line at all.

RISE OF THE DEAD
by Anthony Giangregorio
DEATH IS ONLY THE BEGINNING!

In less than forty-eight hours, more than half the globe was infected.

In another forty-eight, the rest would be enveloped.

The reason?

A science experiment gone horribly wrong which enabled the dead to walk, their flesh rotting on their bones even as they seek human prey.

Jeremy was an ordinary nineteen year old slacker. He partied too much and had done poorly in high school. After a night of drinking and drugs, he awoke to find the world a very different place from the one he'd left the night before.

The dead were walking and feeding on the living, and as Jeremy stepped out into a world gone mad, the dead spotting him alone and unarmed in the middle of the street, he had to wonder if he would live long enough to see his twentieth birthday.

THE CHRONICLES OF JACK PRIMUS
BOOK ONE
by Michael D. Griffiths

Beneath the world of normalcy we all live in lies another world, one where supernatural beings exist. These creatures of the night hunt us; want to feed on our very souls, though only a few know of their existence.

One such man is Jack Primus, who accidentally pierces the veil between this world and the next. With no other choice if he wants to live, he finds himself on the run, hunted by beings called the Xemmoni, an ancient race that sees humans as nothing but cattle. They want his soul, to feed on his very essence, and they will kill all who stand in their way. But if they thought Jack would just lie down and accept his fate, they were sorely mistaken.   He didn't ask for this battle, but he knew he would fight them with everything at his disposal, for to lose is a fate worse than death.

He would win this war, and he would take down anyone who got in his way.

ETERNAL NIGHT: A VAMPIRE ANTHOLOGY

Edited by Anthony Giangregorio

Blood, fangs, darkness and terror...these are the calling cards of the vampire mythos.

Inside this tome are stories that embrace vampire history but seek to introduce a new literary spin on this longstanding fictional monster. Follow a dark journey through cigarette-smoking creatures hunted by rogue angels, vampires that feed off of thoughts instead of blood, immortals presenting the fantastic in a local rock band, to a legendary monster on the far reaches of town.

Forget what you know about vampires; this anthology will destroy historical mythos and embrace incredible new twists on this celebrated, fictional character.

Welcome to a world of the undead, welcome to the world of *Eternal Night*.

DEAD HISTORY 2

A Zombie Anthology

Edited by Anthony Giangregorio

From the dawn of mankind, the walking dead have been with us.

The greatest moments in history are not what they appear.

Through the ages, the undead have been there, only the proof has been erased, documents destroyed, and witnesses silenced.

The living dead is man's greatest secret.

In this tome, are a few of the stories of what really happened all those years ago. History isn't alive, it's dead!

INSIDE THE PERIMETER: SCAVENGERS OF THE DEAD

by Alan Spencer

In the middle of nowhere, the vestiges of an abandoned town are surrounded by inescapably high concrete barriers, permitting no trespass or escape. The town is dormant of human life, but rampant with the living dead, who choose not to eat flesh, but to instead continue their survival by cruder means.

Boyd Broman, a detective arrested and falsely imprisoned, has been transferred into the secret town. He is given an ultimatum: recapture Hayden Grubaugh, the cannibal serial killer, who has been banished to the town, in exchange for his freedom.

During Boyd's search, he discovers why the psychotic cannibal must really be captured and the sinister secrets the dead town holds.

With no chance of escape, Broman finds himself trapped among the ravenous, violent dead. With the cannibal feeding on the animated cadavers and the undead searching for Boyd, he must fulfill his end of the deal before the rotting corpses turn him into an unwilling organ donor.

But Boyd wasn't told that no one gets out alive, that the town is a death sentence. For there is no escape from *Inside the Perimeter*.

PLAYING GOD: A ZOMBIE NOVEL
by Jeffery Dye

It was supposed to be a regeneration virus to help soldiers on the battlefield— regrowing limbs and healing wounds— but a simple act of carelessness unleashed it on an unsuspecting world.

For the virus was not perfected, and once exposed, the host quickly dies, only to rise again as one of the undead.

As countries are quickly overrun, scientists and military teams battle to contain the outbreak.

There is no other option.

If the infection continues to spread, soon the entire globe will be consumed. And perhaps that will be a just punishment for a mankind that dared to try to play God.

DEAD HOUSE: A ZOMBIE GHOST STORY
by Keith Adam Luethke

The old mansion on the edge of town, aptly named Dead House, has a history of blood, pain, and death, but what Victor Leeds knows of this past only scratches the surface of the true horrors within.

But when his girlfriend is attacked by a shadowy figure one rainy night, he soon finds himself caught up in a world where the dead walk and ghostly wraiths abound. And to make matters worse, a pair of serial killers are fulfilling carefully made plans, and when they are done, the small town of Stormville, New York will run red. The last ingredient to open the gates of Hell, and plunge this small upstate town into madness, is rain.

And in Stormville, it pours by the gallons.

DROPPING FEAR
by Mike Catalano

On a dark night 25 years ago, masked maniac Derek Haddonfear went on a bloody rampage... Today, Derek's son, Will, is happily married, but still struggles to distance himself from the harsh memory of his father. He and his wife, Kerri, have been trying to get pregnant for years with zero success. Infertility begins to take its toll on their marriage.

Kerri can't live without becoming a mother and Will can't live seeing his wife so distraught. Upon coming into contact with a doctor working on an experimental fertility drug, a desperate Will and Kerri decide to give him a shot.

What results from the procedure sends Kerri on an uncontrollably violent path that is all too familiar to Will. Is it her hormones? Is it the drug? Or is Will's chilling past coming back to haunt him in the most bizarre of fashions? Regardless, no one will be prepared for the birth of the newest and most unexpected psychotic slasher in the history of horror.

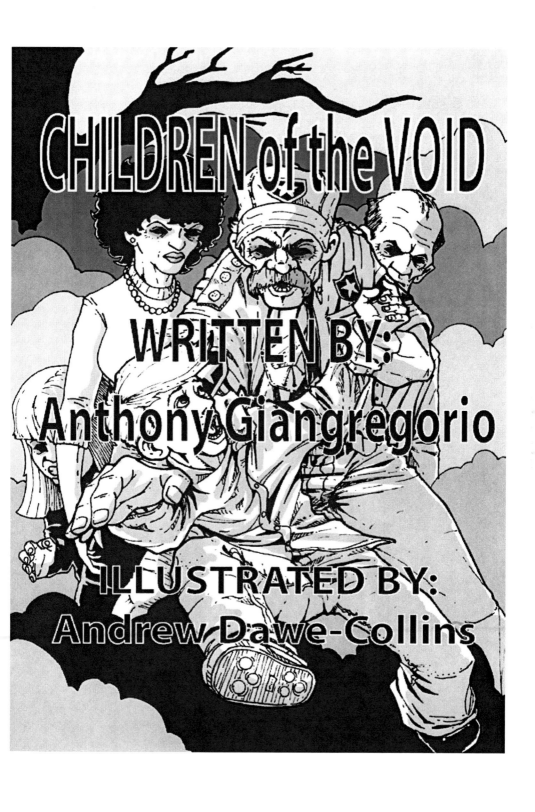

CLAN OF THE BIGFOOT

ANTHONY GIANGREGORIO

THE PLACE TO GO FOR ZOMBIE AND APOCALYPTIC FICTION

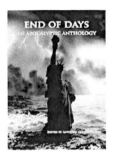
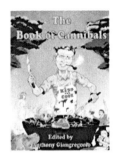
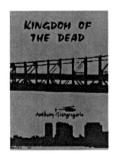

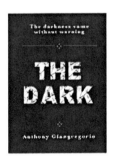

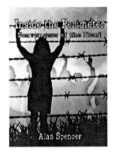

LIVING DEAD PRESS

WHERE THE DEAD WALK
www.livingdeadpress.com

CPSIA information can be obtained at www.ICGtesting.com
Printed in the USA
BVOW040449091111

275671BV00006B/44/P

9 781611 990324